I0645050

She couldn't believe it! How could he betray her like this…

There on the front page was a terrible photo of Tali coming out of her office doors, complete with wig and scarf. But the face was definitely hers.

Tali was in shock for a few seconds. How could this be? How did it happen?

"You're kidding!" She finally found her voice. But now she couldn't think of even one word.

Exclusive photos inside the headline continued. *See why Margaret Barnett isn't who she says she is!*

"Who did this?" she was able to ask. "Who? I want his, or her, head. Immediately. It has to be someone in the building. Someone close enough to be able to take photos."

A mental picture of a handsome young janitor working the hall with toolboxes and a lunch box on the floor around him came to Lily's mind. But she dismissed it as Tali was continuing, giving out orders of what to do about this.

"I certainly hope this rag has good malpractice insurance, 'cause they're going to need it!"

By the end of the day, Tali had the information she wanted.

Brent!

Committed to winning a challenge from friends, he falls in love with a woman who is not what she appears to be…

Brent Walker receives a challenge from friends to interview and photograph Margret Barnett, the elusive heir to a newspaper fortune. His only clue is Granville, a small Southern town. But when he gets there, no one in town will tell him where she lives. Still, all is not lost. While in Granville, he meets and falls in love with Tali, a beautiful young woman who lives on a farm with her grandmother.

She loves him, but she's afraid to let him know who she really is…

Tali is used to people trying to find Margret Barnett, but she knows the town will protect her identity. She's afraid if Brent finds out who she really is, he will only want her money and she wants to be loved for herself. Besides, he's as secretive as she is about his life away from her, and she suspects he's not the humble journalist he appears to be.

Can these two strong-willed people find a common ground of trust and acceptance, or will pride, stubbornness, and deception keep them apart?

KUDOS for *No Small Deceit*

In *No Small Deceit* by Mary Jane Bryan, Tali is a small town farm girl, or so Brent Walker thinks when he meets her. But she isn't what she seems to be. Of course, neither is he. With deceit on both sides, it's hard to have an honest relationship as both parties have something to hide. Add to the deception, the normal male/female misunderstandings and no relationship has much of a chance. But when they both get caught deceiving each other, pride and stubbornness make it hard for either one to forgive. The story is cute and clever, the plot strong, and the characters believable. It's a classic love story with an unusual twist, a very good read. ~ *Taylor Jones, Reviewer*

No Small Deceit by Mary Jane Bryan is just what the title says it is: the story of two people who start a relationship with a little white lie and find that it soon balloons out of control. Love is hard enough when the two people involved are honest with each other. But when you add omissions and deceptions, taking the relationship where you want it to go is nearly impossible. Our heroine, Tali, is a small-town girl, or so she tries to pretend, but her innocent façade is hiding a big secret—she's really a newspaper heiress everyone thinks is an old lady. Into her life walks Brent Walker, humble journalist and mouth-watering gorgeous. But he isn't what he appears to be either. Can these two complicated people wade through the deceit and mistrust to find true love, or are they doomed from the start? *No Small Deceit* is a complicated tale of deception, mistrust, and two people who want to be loved for who they are and not what they have. Add in the machinations of Brent trying to get an interview with the newspaper heiress, and you have a charming, funny, and entertaining story. *~ Regan Murphy, Reviewer*

No Small Deceit

Mary Jane Bryan

A Black Opal Books Publication

DEDICATION

*Thanks to all my friends and
family for their continual patience
with me. I especially want to thank
my husband, Peter, for his persistence
in never letting me give up
on my dreams.*

Chapter 1

Summer 2000:

Tali spotted the man when she was about halfway across the meadow, walking her horse at a slow pace. This was familiar territory for both of them. The man was getting out of the driver's side of a vehicle, the side opposite her. He walked toward the back of the car. He opened the trunk and started rummaging around.

She wondered what he was doing on this rocky, dirt road, and then she grinned to herself. She bet Burt, owner of Burt's Gas and Tire Repair shop on the highway, had probably told this man to turn down this road as a shortcut to get to Granville.

The man had probably asked for the nearest way to Granville.

Since Burt was a great practical joker, he always told people who stopped and asked that to go this way.

Well, Tali thought, *it actually is the closet way to get to Granville in terms of distance, that is true. But, as far as time is concerned, the man just found out the problem.*

As Tali approached the car from the front, she could hear the man talking to himself. She could not make out exactly what he was saying, but she caught the words "flat," "stupid pot-holes," and a couple of other words she decided she would forget she heard.

She brought TD, her horse, to a stop at the front of the car. They had approached quietly, but the man probably would not have heard them, anyway, talking to himself as he was.

Just then a hand reached up, grabbed the top of the open trunk lid, and slammed it down with a loud bang.

He rose up.

"Whoa!" he cried when he saw Tali on TD just a car length away. He took a step backward.

The slamming of the trunk lid and a man suddenly appearing and crying out caused TD to rear up suddenly, which was unusual for him. He was generally a calm horse. Nothing ever seemed to affect him.

Tali barely had time to adjust in the saddle. If she wasn't as excellent a rider as she was, she would have been thrown off at the unexpected move. TD may have reared up because Tali had been so startled when she saw the man, she was sure she jerked the reins backward suddenly. TD was not used to having such a command from her. He probably just reared, confused as to what he was supposed to do.

The man was, by far, the best-looking man she had ever seen in her life. Dark blond hair was cut in an upsweep to frame his handsome face. His blue eyes looked as startled as hers did, she was sure.

Brent, on the other hand, had taken even another step backward. He knew he was looking at the most beautiful woman he had ever seen.

Tali had somewhat recovered her composure and calmed TD, but her heart was still racing. She was sure the man could see it pounding through her T-shirt.

"Flat?" she asked.

She knew the answer, of course. That was the major problem with this road. It seemed every time someone tried to go this way, for whatever reason, the result was a flat. That is, if the person were lucky. A ruined tire was more common. The locals avoided this road as much as possible.

She would have to talk to Burt about telling people to come this way. It simply wasn't fair to them, practical joke or not.

"Yeah," Brent answered, "an elderly gentleman at a gas station told me to come this way and I would be in Granville in 'no time flat.' I guess he was right!"

Brent grinned, sheepishly. He knew the joke was on him. He should have turned back when he was only a few yards down this road. At that time, he could tell what it looked like ahead for as far as he could see. He had hoped it would get better. But it hadn't.

He should have at least turned around at the farmhouse he saw on a hill about a half a mile back.

"I'll have to talk to Burt about that," the woman said.

Brent brought his thoughts back to her. But his thoughts had never really left her. How could they?

"What's that?" he asked.

Tali could have kicked herself. Here was her dream man, obviously from the city and wealthy, also, by the make of his car. And all she could do was say something stupid! He would surely think she was just a "hick from the sticks" and never want to be near her again.

She took a deep breath. She knew she wanted to keep him talking. His voice sent chills down her spine. She had never had such a reaction to any other man before.

Brent wanted to keep her talking. Maybe evasive answers or idiotic questions would keep her here.

"The elderly man you probably asked about how to get to Granville. He thinks it's funny to send people this way. A little ways up the highway, you would have seen a sign at an intersection, with directions on how to get to Granville. It's a very decently-paved county road. Nothing like this."

"I guess I'm just lucky," Brent replied. *In more ways*

than one, he thought, *because I may have never met you otherwise. Here you are, out in the middle of nowhere, the most beautiful woman I've ever seen.*

Tali smiled. Actually, she would thank Burt and give him a big hug the next time she saw him. She had been leisurely walking TD across the meadow, going home, with really nothing to do the rest of the day. Sitting on the porch swing at the farmhouse could only be done for so long.

"I bet he gets lots of tire repairs from sending unsuspecting people this way, right?" he asked, sarcastically. It seemed logical to Brent—send someone to a place where they would have a flat, then offer your services.

"I really don't think he looks at it that way," she responded, bristling at his tone. She had known Burt Madison all her life. It was just his way.

Brent caught the narrowing of her eyes and the almost-resentful tone of her voice. He sure didn't want to offend her, not at this beginning stage of what he hoped would be a delightful relationship.

No, one should not offend such a beautiful woman as this. He didn't want a strike against him from the get-go.

She dropped the subject, much to his relief.

"What's the problem?" she asked. "Can't you fix a tire?"

This time *his* eyes narrowed. What kind of man did she think he was? A wuss?

"Of course I can change a tire, if, and that's a big if, I

have a tire iron, which seems to be missing from this trunk. And, no, I'm not so irresponsible as not to have one. I let a friend borrow my car last weekend, and I do admit I didn't think to look in the trunk to make sure everything was still there when he returned it. He didn't mention having a flat or using the tire iron, but there it is. You just assume everything will be there as you left it."

He was sweating, his forehead covered. His shirt was soaked. He was stuck in the middle of nowhere. And he had just met a beautiful woman looking like this. He was in no mood to be friendly or even courteous. What right did she have to look so cool, to be so happy and friendly?

"Hop up behind me. TD and I'll take you to town. Eddie at the station will bring you back out, fix your flat."

The horse had been prancing, never still, as she made her offer.

Her voice was melodious, a lovely sound.

But Brent had never been on a horse in his life, much less such a magnificent beast as this.

"No way," he said, shaking his head. "Thanks for the offer, but not me."

"Suit yourself," she responded, shrugging.

In one fluid motion, horse and rider turned, crossed the ditch, and jumped up the other side to the open meadow.

"Wait!" Brent called, but his voice fell onto deaf ears.

A second before he called out the horse had sprung into a gallop.

As she galloped across the meadow, she almost forgot about the horse. She had just met the best-looking man she had ever seen. She was still shaking.

Why had she offered to take him to town on her horse? Obviously, he was a "city slicker," and was probably afraid of horses, especially one as big and powerful looking as TD.

ↄ৩৫ↄ

He watched as they crossed the meadow. The horse seemed to glide across the grass, the rider in perfect harmony. They were one.

Her long, beautiful hair flowed out behind her. He watched until they disappeared among the trees.

Then he noticed the silence again.

"That was dumb. Really dumb," he said aloud to himself.

He straightened up. He reached for his cell phone and flipped it open. No service.

Great, he thought. *This must be a "dead zone."*

He tossed the phone onto the front seat of the car.

He was not sure how far it was to town, but he knew that the farmhouse was about a half mile behind, so he decided to go that way. He could telephone for help from there.

He reached into the backseat for his jacket and slung it over one shoulder as he began walking. He wasn't going to reach any town in time to find and try to interview anyone this evening, let alone Mrs. Margaret M. Barnett, heiress to the Quincy fortune and newspaper baroness.

Chapter 2

For the past fifteen minutes, he had been traveling down this rocky dirt road, wondering if there really was a town at the end of it. *Nothing is worth this,* he thought. Maybe he should just forget about the challenge he had picked, fix the flat, and go home.

No, he couldn't do that. A challenge was a challenge. He had never run from anything before.

The yellow and red flowers grew in prolific abundance along the fence on one side of the road. He stood still for a moment with his hands on his hips, surveying the area that circumstances had forced him to stop in, and sighed.

He was on a hard-packed, rocky road. Looking down at his feet, he saw rocks sticking up out of the surface. A little to his right there was a pothole.

He knew about those! He had been trying to dodge those since he had been on this road. At the same time, he had tried not to get too close to the bushes at the sides, their branches spreading out over part of the road. He wasn't interested in scratching his BMW. Otherwise, he could appreciate the beauty and tranquility of the place.

Graceful, stately oak trees stretched in majesty to the sky, their branches intertwined. Spanish moss hung in abundance from the branches, swaying gently in the breeze. He watched as squirrels and birds scampered and hopped from branch to branch, tree to tree. The warbling of different birds filled the air with song. He listened to another sound. He realized what it was. Cicadas were in full "voice." Their music ebbed and flowed in response to the conductor. This "concert master" was a certain cicada that dictated the rhythm of the chorus.

A gentle breeze moved the leaves, producing a faint rustling among the branches. The zephyr provided a refreshing coolness on this hot, muggy summer day.

He sighed, wishing he could enjoy the beauty of the trees and wild flowers. But he had put himself on a timetable, and it was suddenly in danger of being torn apart.

The stillness and calmness of the area brought a certain serenity to his body and mind. He *had* been working too hard lately. He felt he could just stay here, never moving again.

Just as he thought he would never spot the farmhouse,

it finally came into view. It was a good quarter mile up a driveway from the road, nestled on a hill among big, beautiful oaks. Tall, stately pine trees lined the driveway on either side.

As he entered the yard, a huge dog rose up from its position on the bottom step of the porch. An old woman sat in a cane-back chair, snapping beans, putting the ends in a paper bag and the beans in a large pot. He stopped, not quite sure what the dog was going to do.

The dog took a step toward him, wagging its tail. Brent cautiously and slowly reached out a hand and let the dog smell his scent. The animal licked his hand.

The old woman had seemingly paid no mind to this exchange of greeting between man and dog.

But someone else had been watching.

"Well, well, I've never seen him do that before," a familiar voice said.

Brent looked up as a figure opened the screen door and stepped out on to the porch. A figure in cut-off shorts, T-shirt, long hair flowing.

"You!" he said. "What are you doing here?" he asked before he thought.

"Me?" she asked, putting her hand on her chest. "Moi? I live here."

"Live here?"

"Do you always repeat everything in your conversations?" she asked, smiling.

Her smile took his breath away, but her words rankled. She would never know what she did to him. He'd make sure of that.

"Only if I think someone needs it," he replied in kind.

She raised her eyebrow.

"Now, children, hush, now," said the old woman on the porch.

They turned toward her.

"This is Granny Mae. My name's Tali," the girl said.

"I'm Brent. Brent Walker. Do you have a phone I can use?" he asked, as he hung his jacket over the porch railing. "And, by the way, you've never seen what before?"

"Oh, just Duke, there," she said, gesturing toward the dog, who had now laid back down, at Brent's feet. "Duke usually greets strangers with fierce barks and growls. I have no idea why he didn't bark at you."

"Told you so," Granny said.

"Now, Granny!"

Brent looked from one to the other. This conversation was lost on him.

"Matchmaker," Tali said, simply, with a grin.

"Oh!" Brent exclaimed, not sure what to say to that.

Matchmaker? This beautiful girl didn't need any help there. The only thing Brent could imagine was that perhaps there were no eligible young men around here.

"Phone?" he asked again, getting back to the business at hand.

"No phone," she said, spreading her hands.

"You're kidding," he said, then cursed himself for not bringing his cell phone from the car. It might not even be there when he got back to his vehicle. Having been so hot, sweaty, and frustrated, he didn't even think about it until now.

Smiling at the look on his face, almost as if reading his mind, she pointed toward the road.

He turned in the direction she was pointing. An old pickup came into view.

"Eddie," she said. "I rode into town earlier and told him about you. He said he'd come. If Eddie says he'll do something, he will. Never doubt that."

The old pickup came to a stop in front of them, and a young man stuck his head out the window.

"Well, come on. I don't like to be out after dark," he said.

"Not out—" Brent began, but one look at Tali's face had him grabbing his jacket and heading toward the truck.

"Go to Fran's Bed and Breakfast for the night," Tali called after him. "Tell her I sent you."

Brent acknowledged that he had heard her with a wave of his hand as Eddie jockeyed the pickup around in the yard and headed back down the lane that served as a driveway.

Brent waved out the window and watched in the side view mirror as she returned it.

On the porch, Granny nodded. "Yep, he's the one," she said, smiling.

Tali said nothing in reply. She simply turned and went back into the house, giving no indication she had even heard Granny's remark.

Chapter 3

They made it to Eddie's service station with the flat tire at dusk, but it was dark as Brent knocked on the front door of Fran's Bed and Breakfast. A sign had instructed him to "Please Knock," which seemed strange to him. Used to the major hotels around the world, knocking for entrance seemed very strange.

A middle-aged woman opened the door.

"Yes?" she asked.

"Good evening, ma'am," he began, with a smile. This smile usually allowed him to get his way.

She nodded, agreeing.

"A young lady named Tali said to tell you she sent me. I had a flat outside town and need a room for the night."

As if the name Tali were a magic word, at the mention

of it, Fran had stepped back, inviting him in. She was all smiles. "If Tali sent you, that's fine with me, then," she said. "I have a good room, and you're just in time to wash up before supper."

She looked pointedly at his smudged arms and even at his face.

"Oh, no," he groaned, when he looked at himself in the mirror in his room. He had a large smudge of dirt down the left side of his face.

"I'm sure that really impressed Tali."

His usually impeccably starched shirt was rumpled and sweat-stained.

He cleaned up and enjoyed a delicious meal, one of the best he'd ever eaten. He couldn't tell Fran enough how much he enjoyed it.

No one was in a hurry to leave this woman's table. Better to let that blueberry cobbler settle with a last cup of coffee.

"So, Brent, what brings you to Granville?" a man asked. "Usually a person has to be coming here to get here. It's not like we're on the Interstate."

"You can say that again," Brent said, smiling, but they seemed to know he meant no offense. "Actually, I'm here to try to interview the most elusive woman of wealth in the world, it seems. No one yet has been able to see and talk with Mrs. Margaret M. Barnett, so I thought I might try my hand at it."

For some reason he did not feel the need to explain about his challenge.

He felt a change in the atmosphere. It seemed to drop a degree or two. At the mention of this name, several around the table reached for their coffee cups, busying themselves with drinking.

"More coffee, anyone?" Fran asked, rising from her chair. She headed for the kitchen.

What did I say? Brent wondered.

One older man, who Brent had learned lived at this place on a permanent basis, spoke up. "You won't get to her, young man," he said. "She doesn't allow any visitors out at her place. And I might as well warn you, as we all would—" He paused, looking around the table at the others, who were nodding. "—that no one around these parts will give you any information about her. Might as well not ask. We're all pretty protective where our little Margaret's concerned."

"Can't you just point me in the general direction of her house? Surely there aren't so many houses in this town that I couldn't find it."

They just looked at him and again sipped their coffee. He dropped the subject as Fran returned with the coffee pot.

Brent had enough sense not to pursue it at this time.

The next morning, he stepped out onto the screened-in porch that ran around the front and two sides of this building. A swing hung from the ceiling on one end of the porch, rocking chairs were along the wall. Between two of the rocking chairs, in two different spots, a wooden barrel had been placed with care. Checkerboards complete with checkers, sat on top of the barrels. One of the checkerboards had a game in progress, some checkers on the board and some stacked off the board.

He stretched, pushing his hands up in the air above his head. He had just slept like a baby, having gone to sleep as soon as he lay down. The bed had been wonderfully soft.

He glanced around. This small town had the typical Southern "square." An old building in the middle was now a restaurant, called The Old Post Office. It could well have been the original post office for this town.

He was amazed. Although this was the year 2000, time seemed to have stood still here. Except for a few vehicles, this square could be on a 1950s postcard.

Norman Rockwell would appreciate this, he thought.

As he started down the steps to go see about his car, he spotted TD on the other side of the square, tied loosely to a lamppost.

TD could only mean one thing.

Tali!

He felt the excitement the thought of seeing her brought to him.

At that moment, she came out of a shop, her arms full of plastic bags. She was laughing with the shopkeeper, who had followed her out to the sidewalk.

Brent heard her happy laugh, carried on the wind, as he started across the square in long, graceful strides. More than one head turned to watch him as he crossed the short distance.

Tali was saying something to the man, laughing. She spotted Brent at the same time.

TD also spotted him and gave a soft nicker, as if in greeting.

Tali looked quickly over at the horse, surprise registering on her face.

"You, too?" she asked the horse.

The horse tossed its head, shaking its mane, and looked at her.

"Traitor," she said. She turned to watch Brent cross the last street to arrive at her side. *What a good-looking man,* she thought. *Too bad he's so full of himself, he can't even be nice!*

She started arranging the bags, which had handles, onto TD's saddle.

"Good morning," he said from behind her.

Brent had seen her looking at him, so there was no use for her to pretend she didn't know he was there.

She was so beautiful, looking so fresh this morning. He wanted to reach out and turn her around, pull her to him, and kiss her. He did lean toward her, taking a deep breath. He knew she would smell as clean and beautiful as she looked. Her thick hair was pulled back in a ponytail.

"Is it?" she asked, sounding cooler than she had planned.

What was it about this man that made her so testy? Seeing him walking this way had reminded her of yesterday, when she had watched him from behind the screen door at the farm. As he walked up the steps, she had experienced an almost uncontrollable urge to step out to greet him, run into his arms, and put her face up for his kiss. The urge had happened again when she walked out the door and he had taken a step toward her. But he had drawn back, so she did.

What had come over her, anyway? She had met many men in her young life. She had never wanted to run into their arms as she did with this man. True, she had thought about him all night, unable to sleep. She hadn't been prepared to see him first thing this morning.

"Isn't it?" he countered.

"If you say so," she said, as she swung up and into the saddle. She pulled TD's head around and moved away. "Better see about your precious car."

She left him standing there, staring after her, as she cantered down the street and around a corner.

Why was she so prickly? Just because he hadn't wanted to ride with her on the horse? He hadn't done anything to her that he could remember. In fact, he had felt yesterday on the front porch of the farmhouse that she wanted to come to him, and he had almost held out his arms, encouraging her. But they both had turned away at the same time—he because he refused to let her know how she affected him. He wasn't about to try to guess why she did anything.

A movement at the end of the block caught his attention. Eddie was opening his service station. Brent walked down the street, greeting people as he went. People were sure friendly in this small Southern town. They opened their shops early. It wasn't quite seven a.m., yet they were here, setting items outside their doors.

Eddie took the time to examine the tire but then had bad news. He couldn't fix it and didn't have one to match it in stock. It had a special tread. He offered to put a different type on the car, which would get Brent to Springfield, but ride rough. Or, he was willing to go to Springfield to replace the tire. He needed other supplies, anyway.

But he explained that if Brent planned on going to Tali's very often while he was here, the temporary balloon tire would not last on those potholes and rocks in that road. It would be better to have a new tire to match the others.

Brent was surprised when he found himself agreeing to let Eddie go to Springfield, probably not until the next day. That meant Brent would spend the night here again.

Why would he want to spend any extra time in this small town? Why not just get the interview and leave?

He already knew the answer. The picture of a petite, feisty red-head atop a beautiful horse came to mind.

He refused to let her image stay there.

"Since we have to wait on this, can you tell me how to

get to Margaret Barnett's house?" Brent asked, in what he hoped was a casual tone. He wanted to sound like he was just asking how to get to the town library.

Eddie didn't answer. He picked up the phone book, intent on finding and calling a place that had the required tire.

Brent knew, however, that he had heard him.

Brent waited. When he knew Eddie wasn't going to give an answer, he asked, "Why won't anyone in this town tell me where Mrs. Barnett lives?"

Eddie looked up, but before he could answer, another voice spoke up from the office doorway. "Because everyone is very protective of her, which she appreciates very much."

Brent looked up to see Tali standing there. The light from the garage bay outlined her figure in such a way that it took his breath away.

"No one has ever interviewed her. What makes you think you can?" she asked.

He smiled. "Charm. Wit. Good looks. You name it!"

His tone said that he usually got by with this banter, giving him a natural inroad to start a conversation. Most women smiled and relaxed.

Not Tali. "Oh?" she asked.

She did not smile, but looked at him very seriously.

His smile faded.

What did it take with this woman? How could such a beautiful creature be so cold?

"Found one!" Eddie proclaimed, hanging up the phone.

Brent and Tali continued looking at each other.

"Hey," Eddie said, walking up to Brent and touching his sleeve.

"And why is everyone so protective of her?" Brent asked. "She's worth billions, owns a major newspaper chain, and she's supposed to really be a character. She's probably very interesting. It would make a good article for several national, even international, publications."

"So, you *are* a reporter. I thought so."

She started to turn away, in disgust, it seemed.

"No," he said, reaching for and taking her arm as she turned, forcing her to turn back to him. "No, I'm not a journalist," he said, still holding her arm.

She looked down at his hand on her arm then back up to him, raising her eyebrow.

"Sorry," he said, as he let her go.

"Then, what?" she asked. "Do you want some grant money for a pet cause, or something? It seems—Margaret—is always being hit on for money for something."

"Margaret, is it? Then you do know her? Personally?"

"Oh, yes, I know her," she responded. "Everyone in town knows her. That's why they try to protect her from the likes of you."

"Likes of me?" he asked. "And what does she, or anyone here, for that matter, know about me? How can she or they get to know me, if I don't get the opportunity to even see her?"

Tali looked at him steadily. "Tell you what," she said, "why don't you write out the list of questions you would like to ask her, and I'll that see she gets them. If she wants to answer, I'll bring them back to you. If she doesn't, then you won't see her, anyway."

Eddie had been sitting on a stool a few feet away, listening, obviously enjoying this exchange. He had a big grin on his face.

"Is that the best I can do?" Brent asked. "I'm sure if she would just see me for a minute, we could set up an interview. I mean, how do I know it would be her, and not just anyone, answering the questions?"

"Think she would fall for your…charm, is it?" Tali asked, mockingly.

"Yes, just like you have," he countered.

"Me?" she asked. "Me? If you think I'm impressed by your super ego, then you can just…just…"

She was so indignant, she couldn't finish her sentence.

She turned and flounced out of the office, her long, full ponytail swishing back and forth. Her hands were clenched at her sides. Brent stared after her. He wanted to run after her, turn her around, pull her to him, kiss her, and never let her go. But instead he just stood there.

"Way to go," said Eddie, still grinning.

"Huh?" Brent asked, looking over at him. "Did you say something?"

"She likes you, I can tell," Eddie replied.

"Likes me?" Brent questioned. "Are you kidding? I think she'd like to scratch my eyes out. There goes my interview, or even answers to questions, from Margaret Barnett."

"Don't bet on it," Eddie responded.

"What do you mean?" Brent asked.

Eddie just shrugged. "Stranger things have happened. You ready? Want to ride with me over to Springfield, pick up that tire you need?"

"Which way do you go?" Brent asked. "Can you drop me off at Tali's house and pick me up on the way back?"

"Sure. You a glutton for punishment or something?"

"There must be a way of getting through to her," he said.

Eddie laughed. "Which one? Margaret or Tali?" he asked.

"Either. Both," was Brent's reply.

Now, it had become a challenge, a vendetta. Even if he didn't get to see Margaret Barnett, he was determined to have Tali eating out of his hand before he had to leave Granville.

He wasn't used to being rebuffed by any woman.

He wasn't about to start now!

Chapter 4

Eddie stopped at the end of the driveway to let Brent out. Brent had asked to be dropped off there, so Eddie could get to Springfield and back as soon as possible. They had been delayed at the service station when a man had brought his pickup in, the motor threatening to die every time the vehicle came to a stop. Eddie had taken the time to check it out, get it running smoother, and idling correctly.

Brent saw Granny sitting on the porch before he was halfway up the drive. He heard a familiar sounding motor start up but couldn't tell what direction it was coming from. He stopped to listen, looking around at the sky.

In a minute or two, a helicopter came into view over the top of the house. He only caught a glimpse of it before it dropped down again below the roofline. He heard it fade into the distance.

In that brief glimpse, something about the helicopter looked very familiar but he just couldn't place it. It must have flown in from the east and then banked north. The farmhouse faced the south, situated on a knoll. The ground sloped gently away behind the house, but he couldn't see anything over the ridge. At thick stand of trees prevented anyone seeing beyond them.

Although the helicopter and its markings nagged at him, he temporarily dismissed it from his mind.

"Back again, huh?" Granny said by way of greeting. "Tali ain't here. She's gone to town."

"I know," he said.

She looked up at him quickly, sharply. She relaxed when he continued.

"I saw her earlier at Eddie's station. It sure is peaceful out here," he said, seemingly dismissing the subject of Tali.

The old woman wasn't fooled, and they both knew it. Why else would he be back out here, if not to see Tali? It wasn't to see her, Granny knew that for sure. But she kept quiet, willing to let him do the talking. She had learned long ago that you learned more by listening than by talking.

He only sat a minute more before he asked, "Mind if I look around? Maybe look in the barn? I haven't been to many farms before. Actually, I haven't been to any," he admitted with a grin.

Granny smiled back at him, showing toothless gums.

At least I can still charm someone! he thought.

"Sure, go ahead. Just don't bother TD. Tali gets real upset if anyone touches him, almost. 'Course, he may not let you touch him. Right spirited, that one is."

"You can say that again!" exclaimed Brent.

They both knew he wasn't talking about the horse.

Chapter 5

Tali looked out and down as the helicopter headed north, toward Springfield and the airport there. From there her private jet would take her to Atlanta.

Tomorrow morning was the annual stockholders' meeting. She had the afternoon and evening to prepare herself for it.

Her speech to the stockholders was more or less a pep talk, a morale booster. They liked to see her. Although she kept her finger on the pulse of her corporation and knew at any moment what was happening, for the last two days she had not been able to think of anything but Brent Walker.

She closed her eyes and remembered the first time she saw him. Of course, she had heard him before she saw him.

She had spotted the black car on the road from across the open field. TD had moved silently through the meadow, across the ditch, to stop in front of the BMW. Obviously, the man had a flat tire and he was frantically searching for something in the trunk.

She heard him cursing under his breath when he couldn't find what he was looking for.

He had slammed the truck down so hard she had jumped, causing TD to rear up prance sideways. He was so in tune with her every movement that her jump had startled him, also.

She had also felt herself draw in her breath and tense up when the man looked up at her, as startled as she was.

He was gorgeous!

Large blue eyes had stared at her from beneath long, thick lashes.

Lashes to die for. Even hers weren't that long!

How many women would envy those lashes, a natural asset to this man's good looks.

Since he was obviously a visitor to the area, she had been prepared to offer what help she could to him. Her offer of riding with her on TD to town was unusual. To many it would have been an honor, yet he had seemingly scorned it.

For some reason, that had angered her, causing her to feel rejected, a feeling she was not familiar with and didn't like.

But what shook her most was the fact she had not been

able to get him off her mind, not even for a minute, since that first moment.

But she had her pride, too. He would never know how she felt!

In spite of her thoughts returning time and time again to Brent, Tali was able to concentrate enough throughout the evening to know what she would say the next morning in her speech.

From helicopter to jet to helicopter, she was now cozily entrenched in her private penthouse on the top floor of her corporation's main office building.

Unique in its design and conception, she'd had the building constructed so that her personal helicopter was able to be lowered completely down into the building, out of sight, and the door would close above it. At that point, from the air or roof, no evidence of a helo pad was in sight. The other half of this top floor was her penthouse and the apartment of her secretary and lifelong BFF, Lily.

Tali finally laid her notes aside, feeling confident that she knew their contents.

Her thoughts returned to Brent.

How dare he think he could charm his way into her presence? And for an interview, at that. She had never granted reporters personal interviews, and she wasn't about to start with him.

In fact, early on in her career, with the knowledge that she would someday be chairperson of the corporation, she had vowed to stay out of the public eye. She had well-educated, competent managers that she fully trusted to run her business interests. She felt no need to flaunt her wealth.

She never forgot her mother's family, the town she was born in, or the people there. For this reason, the citizens of Granville loved her and helped protect her privacy. She acted like one of them when she was there, which was often, and she was accepted completely.

Her money had helped put many of the young people through college and get them started in their chosen careers.

She was simply "Tali" to them, and Tali she would remain. Her grandfather, Granny Mae's husband, had given her the nickname when she was born. It had stuck, of course, like all nicknames tend to do.

He had said that Margaret Matilda was too hard for such a dainty thing to handle, so he had shortened the Matilda to Tali.

She was glad he had. The name Margaret Matilda may have been in her mother's family for generations, but she didn't think she would pass it on—when, or if, she ever had children.

Unbidden, beautiful blue eyes, long lashes, and Adonis features came to mind, crowding out all other thoughts. She found herself wondering what their children would look like, and couldn't believe she was having such thoughts.

What children? She laughed to herself. *He obviously couldn't stand me on sight and I certainly couldn't put up with such an arrogant, egotistical man!* She snuggled down in her bed and went to sleep on thoughts of curly-haired, blue-eyed babies.

Chapter 6

As Brent walked up the driveway, Granny Mae thought what a fine-looking man this stranger was. He was almost as good looking as her Hank had been at that age. What memories the sight of this young man of Tali's brought back to her.

And there was no doubt in her mind that this young man already belonged to Tali.

She had watched as they bristled at each other, one barely talking civilly to the other. Yet, Granny could tell there was a mutual attraction so strong, so immediate, between these two that, if they both had not denied it, they would have been in each other's arms. For a second, at one point the other day, she though that it was going to happen, anyway. But they both drew back at the same time.

She had felt that, too.

They'd come around, she knew.

She watched him as he walked to the barn. He had broad, powerful shoulders atop a slim, trim torso. He obviously kept himself in top physical shape. He was full of pride, just as her Hank had been at that age, and always, really.

That's what made men like this the way they were. They had such fierce pride in themselves and their accomplishments. They never let anything take that away from them, not even the all-consuming, unconditional love they gave to the woman they finally chose to love. And these women allowed them to keep that pride.

Tali was a match for him, Granny knew, but he would remain an independent man, just as Tali would remain an independent woman.

Brent approached the open door of the barn. Granny had given him permission to explore the farm. A variety of aromas assaulted his senses. Fresh hay was the most prominent, causing him to sneeze.

A soft nicker answered his sneeze, letting him know that TD was in the barn. After his eyes adjusted to the dimness, he saw the horse at the side, his head above the boards of his stall, as if he were waiting to greet Brent.

Brent went to the horse. He did not remember Granny's warning about touching him. The horse seemed to welcome him stroking its nose.

"I thought Tali would be here," he said out loud to the horse. "Do you miss her, too?"

The horse shook his head, seemingly in response to Brent's question. He was used to Tali leaving him alone for several days at a time, but, yes, if he could think in human terms, he would have felt he missed her. TD and Tali had a bond between them that few humans and horses did.

An open door at the side of the barn allowed TD to go outside and get his exercise whenever he wanted. An open pasture stretched out from the barn.

Brent spent some time exploring the barn and tack room. He found a litter of kittens in some hay and the mother cat allowed him to pet them for a while. Then he wandered outside. As he passed down the side of the barn, TD joined him at the fence, again nickering.

"I know, I miss her, too, and I've only known her for one day. Am I crazy, or what?"

A fence along the back of the property enclosed the cleared yard. A gate in the fence allowed a person to go through to a path in the woods, but this gate was padlocked.

Brent thought it strange for this farm to have a high chain-link fence with barbed wire around the top, and a locked gate.

Fences had always intrigued him. He speculated as to why property owners put them up. Of course, some reasons were obvious, such as TD's enclosure.

But why this? What, or who, was it keeping out?

It never occurred to Brent to wonder if people were to stay on the house side of the fence. He thought, as most would, that the locked gate was intended to keep prowlers or hunters on the forest side, preventing them from getting too close to the house. The padlock hung down in the middle, so that it could be locked or opened from either side. But Brent saw no significance in this.

After returning to the porch, he learned from Granny that Tali might be gone for several days.

So she wasn't just in Granville.

Granny wouldn't say where she was, though. He asked her about Margaret Barnett. Granny just shook her head.

"I really couldn't say," she replied.

Couldn't, or wouldn't, Brent wondered.

"Come on in the kitchen and have some lemonade," Granny said.

Brent followed her into the house.

"Have a look around the living room while I get the lemonade," Granny said. "There are some photos of Tali when she was younger."

Brent stopped at the living room door. There was an old-fashioned console TV with a VCR box on top of it. A swivel VCR stand was full of cartridges. He knew many people in the Southern countryside, especially older people, still used their VCRs.

Wal-Mart still sold blank VCR tapes so people could record their favorite TV shows or movies. The retail giant still sold VCR machines. They knew there was still a market for these.

He saw a rotary box on the table beside a well-worn recliner.

He recognized this as a rotary box because his grandmother still had one, to turn her TV antennae that stood on the house. Yes, he'd seen an antennae on this house, but had not thought about it at the time.

Looking around, he spotted several framed photos on a side table. He picked up one of Tali as a cheerleader, in the traditional pose with one pom-pom in the air.

She hasn't changed much, he thought.

Granny returned with the lemonade, gesturing for him to sit down.

"Have patience, young man," she said. "You know what they say. Good things come to those who wait."

He opened his mouth to answer, but was spared having to respond by a series of honks.

Eddie had returned.

Chapter 7

Brent was sitting on a stool at the cafe counter. Eddie had put the new tire on his car, but Brent was not through in Granville. He would do all he could to see Margaret Barnett. His coffee cup was halfway to his mouth when he heard the familiar "chop-chop" of helicopter blades.

He jumped down, splashing coffee on the counter as he lowered the cup. He pushed through the door. Stepping clear of buildings and trees, he looked up in the direction from which the sound was coming.

It flew low over town, heading east. Just as he had thought at Tali's.

He *had* seen that helo before! Now, he remembered. It was Margaret Barnett's personal helicopter. He could see

the flaming red and yellow emblem of her publishing corporation painted on the side.

But was it coming or going? Was Mrs. Barnett leaving
town or arriving?

He decided to get his car and follow the helo. Maybe he
could keep it in sight. However, by the time he had reached
his car parked behind the boarding house, there was no
sound of the chopper anywhere.

He stopped his car on the edge of town, wondering
where to go next.

This town was a curious one. Everyone he had asked
for information about Margaret Barnett had been very close-
lipped. They really did protect her. And somehow he knew
offering to pay for any information would just set him back
even further with these people.

He found himself turning up the country road to Tali's
before he realized what he had done.

Halfway up the drive, he saw a large horse trailer and
dual axle pickup parked in front of the barn. The pickup and
trailer matched in color, a beautifully coordinated pair. He
parked and walked over to where Tali was helping a man
put TD in the trailer.

She glanced at him, noting his presence, but was busy
with TD.

To its credit, the horse was calmly going up the ramp
into the horse trailer. And what a trailer it was. It was top-
of-the-line for conveying horses from place to place.

Tali had climbed in with TD. Brent could hear her talking to the horse.

In a few minutes, she jumped out, removed the ramp, shut and latched the door. She took a few steps backward, putting herself in full view of the driver, and waved at him.

This gave Brent an opportunity to watch her. As before, he caught his breath.

She was wearing a T-shirt and cutoff jeans. The T-shirt showed off her full breasts in vivid detail. He felt his excitement mount as he watched her.

Every time he saw her, no matter what she was wearing, he wanted to reach out and pull her close to him. He knew it would be heaven to have his arms around her.

"All ready to go," she said to the driver. "See you in few days."

"Take it easy, Miss Tali," he responded. "And don't worry about Tandy Dan, now."

"I won't" she promised. "I know he's in good hands."

The driver smiled, pleased with the compliment.

She stuck her hands in her pockets as she watched the rig go down the drive.

Tandy Dan? The horse? Brent was thinking. *Tandy Dan? Now, where had he heard that name before?*

That was it!

He turned to Tali, who looked forlorn, still watching the pickup as it drove out of sight.

"TD?" he asked. "Tandy Dan?"

She looked over at him and nodded.

"There was a Tandy Dan who won the Triple Crown several years back—six years, maybe."

Again, she nodded.

"You don't mean—" He couldn't finish.

"Yes, TD is Tandy Dan." She smiled. "I always feel like this when he goes away, even though I know it will only be for a few days. I still miss him, though. I like to think he misses me, too."

She flashed him that beautiful smile that made his heart skip a beat.

"Anyone would miss you," he said, softly.

But she had turned away and did not catch what he said.

She turned back.

"What did you say?"

"Nothing, really," he replied. "It can't be the same horse," he said, continuing the thought.

"It can't?" Tali asked in reply.

"No way. *That* Tandy Dan would be worth…oh…at least…millions, maybe," he said, with a wave of his hand.

"Well, he wasn't cheap," agreed Tali.

"Do you train him?" Brent asked. He couldn't allow himself to think she might own him. How could she? Sure, this was a nice farm, as country places go, but it was just that—a country home. No one of such modest-looking means could afford a horse like Tandy Dan.

"If you mean train him for racing, then the answer is no," replied Tali. "But I do take very good care of him. He has accepted me and treats me as a friend, and that's all we can hope for from anyone or anything, isn't it? Besides," she continued, "how much training does it take to be a stud? I thought that came natural for all males."

She was smiling at him, teasing him.

He took a step toward her and she was in his arms before they both realized or could stop themselves. She raised her head to tell him to let her go, but she realized too late that it was a mistake.

He immediately bent his head and kissed her, slowly, passionately. No one had ever kissed her like this before! She found her arms around him, holding herself up, lest she faint, she felt so weak.

Finally, he drew away, looking down at her triumphantly.

That was his mistake. She pushed him away, not willing to admit what his kiss did to her. She was trembling, so she put her hands back in her pockets.

"At least, I thought it came natural for all males," she said. Unable to accept the emotions and thoughts he aroused in her, she felt a need to lash out at him, hurt him. She knew insulting his male ego would do it.

"Doesn't it?" he asked, laughing. He was undaunted.

She gave him a hard look, a look that had caused most men she had met to back down, and leave her alone. She turned and walked toward the barn, her back stiff with anger.

He stood and watched her walk away. It was hard for him to take his eyes off her. What a kiss! So there *was* fire beneath all that ice. Maybe she had just never met any man yet to match her passion and desire. By her actions and what she said, though, she couldn't stand him.

Yet her response to his kiss was overwhelming. He found himself shaking, but would never admit it, just as he knew she wouldn't.

He wouldn't be bested. It was now a personal challenge. He would make her love him, fall for him, and then walk away from her, just as he had all the women he had known before.

He turned toward the house, catching sight of Granny standing on the porch, watching them.

She was smiling.

Chapter 8

"Mrs. Barnett, Mrs. Barnett!" Lily called to Tali. Tali had been attempting to walk down the hall, past the door to her office, but Lily, her secretary, called out to her.

Tali turned into her outer office. She smiled at Lily, wondering what was happening. Lily wasn't very excitable, and her best asset was her ability to shield Tali from unwanted calls. Most callers just simply did not get past Lily to get to Tali.

Apart from her talents as a secretary, she was also Tali's best friend, had been since they were both in the second grade. She had an apartment, as part of her salary package, on the thirtieth floor of this building, the same floor as Tali's penthouse.

"What's so urgent?" Tali asked.

"There's a man on the line, asking for Margaret Barnett," she began.

Tali waited, looking at her friend. That was nothing unusual.

"He says he knows Tali, a friend of yours. That he *knows* you would like to talk with him."

"Name?" asked Tali, beginning to suspect who was on the line.

"Brent Walker," came the reply.

Tali wasn't surprised.

"You know him?" asked Lily.

"You might say that," Tali replied. The picture of a beautiful, blue-eyed man had come to mind. Tali wondered if her burning cheeks were showing as she remembered the feel of his lips on hers.

They were showing. Lily noticed the change in Tali at the mention of this man's name. Lily also wondered why she even had put him on hold, offering to check with Tali or "Mrs. Barnett." She had done it without thinking as she caught a glimpse of Tali coming.

Who was he? she wondered. No name before had invoked such a response from Tali.

"I'll take the call. Put the muffler on, okay?"

Lily just stared at her as Tali walked into her inner office. Not only was Tali already late for the meeting she was heading to when Lily stopped her, but she simply did *not*—

had not ever—taken unsolicited calls like this.

As she moved to switch on the muffler, she knew she would be quizzing Tali very thoroughly this evening about this man.

The "muffler" was the term they used to refer to the electronic equipment that would muffle and distort Tali's voice, making her voice seem huskier and older than she really sounded in person. That was the reason most thought "Mrs. Barnett" was an older woman.

"Margaret Barnett here," Tali said, in her best professional voice. This voice was usually intimidating.

How did Tali know Brent would be unaffected by her cold, impersonal tone?

The ego of the man was unbearable!

"Mrs. Barnett. Hello. My name's Brent Walker. We have a mutual friend from Granville, so I was hoping you would speak with me."

"You'll have to talk fast. I'm already late for a meeting. And who is our mutual friend?"

Tali couldn't stop herself. She was curious as to what Brent would say about Tali, how he would describe and characterize their association.

"Friend" was not quite the term she would use.

The man was unscrupulous. Using an acquaintance like this, hoping it would give him an inroad to someone else.

"A Miss Tali," he responded brightly.

He didn't include the last name and it suddenly dawned

on her that she had not used her last name that day on the porch. So, unless he had asked someone in town, he didn't even know her last name.

"Tali Perkins?" she asked, giving a false last name. *Let's see how he handles this.*

"Must be the same," he said. "Gorgeous auburn hair, beautiful figure and smile, petite, no bigger than a minute?"

Tali drew in her breath. Did he really think she was beautiful? Did he really like her hair, think she was slim?

"That's her," Tali said, her voice breathless. "What can I do for you, Mr. Walker?"

"I know you've never done it before, but would you grant me an interview? Please! I'll get down on my knees and beg, if it helps. See, I'm down."

His tone was teasing, coaxing, knowing it often solicited the type of response he wanted.

In spite of herself, she smiled, picturing him on his knees. So, he could act humble, if it suited his purposes.

She decided to string him along for a while. She would enjoy seeing him squirm, waiting for what he wanted.

"You know what?" she began, "As you know, I never have given anyone an interview, but I'll consider it in your case. That's consider it, only, understand. I'll just think about it. Could you call me back tomorrow afternoon?"

"You bet!" he said.

She could picture his pleased smile, thinking he had accomplished this much with his charm.

"Your minute's up. Good-bye, Mr. Walker."

She hung up the phone and swung around in her chair, facing the large window, looking out over the city. But she didn't see a thing.

Just hearing his voice had created a feeling within her, she didn't want there. She refused to let him affect her this way.

She continued staring out the window, her thoughts on him.

"Tali?" Lily asked from the doorway. "You're late for your meeting."

"Oh!" Tali exclaimed.

She grabbed the portfolio she had placed on the corner of her desk and rushed out of the office.

She left Lily standing there, staring after her, unable to move.

Tali just didn't act this way.

Who was this guy, anyway?

Chapter 9

When he called back the next afternoon, he was in for a big disappointment. Mrs. Barnett had left the city unexpectedly that morning. No, she had left no message for him. Her secretary said she was sure Mrs. Barnett would not forget him, but would be in touch soon.

He hung up the phone, feeling at odds with himself.

Playing a hunch, he decided to go back to Granville. He didn't think she left town because of him, yet maybe she went "home."

Besides, Tali was there, and this gave him a good excuse for going there, just "happening to be there."

Did he need an excuse to go there?

Wasn't being drawn to beauty a reason within itself?

✄✄

Granny wasn't surprised to see him.

Yet, Brent was so busy looking around, especially toward the barn, that her calmness passed him by.

"Tali?" he asked.

"Down yonder," Granny responded, nodding toward the barn.

Brent's long legs took him quickly to the barn door and he heard Tali's voice, talking to TD.

So, the horse was back. Why did he feel he was competing with a horse?

Because the horse has her attention and affection, a small voice told him, *and that's what you want.*

The horse saw him before Tali did. TD gave a soft nicker.

Tali whirled around. "You! What are you doing here?" she asked, before she could stop herself. *Oh, great, what an exciting thing to say. He'll think I'm the dullest person he's ever had to talk to.*

"Just thought I'd see how TD made out," he said.

"Oh?" she asked. "Thought maybe you could swap stories, that sort of thing? Love 'em and leave 'em, huh?"

She was smiling, teasing him.

Brent smiled back at her, drinking in her beauty. It was good to see her smile.

"Well, you have to play the field, you know, until you

find the right one," he said. "You never know where Ms. Perfect may be found."

For no reason, she felt her cheeks grow hot. She turned back to the horse, hiding her face from him.

"And have you found the right one?" she asked, trying to sound casual.

"Yes, I have," he replied.

"Really? And who's the lucky lady?" she asked.

"Well, she's a beauty. High-strung, sort of like TD here." He reached up to stroke the horse. "She's a real thoroughbred. Temper to match it, too. But she's not untamable, she just doesn't know it yet."

Tali laughed. "Are you describing a person or a horse?"

"You do have to tame them both, it seems."

"Oh, you think that's important?" she asked, throwing him a warning glance, which he chose to ignore.

"What?"

"That a woman be 'tame,' as you put it."

"To a degree. But I like an independent woman, too."

"I suppose your fiancée is wealthy, right?"

"She seems to have enough," he replied, looking her up and down, his eyes shining.

He gave her a look that made her cheeks burn. She was glad for the dimness of the barn, the shadows that covered her blush.

He didn't correct her impression that he was engaged. Why not string her along for a while?

At that moment, Granny appeared in the barn door, a picnic hamper in her hands.

Brent hurried to take it from her.

"I thought you two might like to take your lunch down by the creek. I made fried chicken and a chocolate cake this morning."

"Umm, how did you know those are two of my favorite things?" Brent asked.

"You're a man, aren't you?" Granny asked.

Brent laughed. He looked at Tali.

She smiled back at him. "Sure, let's go. The creek is one of my favorite places. Let's go on TD. He loves it there, also."

Brent looked over at the horse. He was apprehensive about getting on the animal.

"You'll be fine," Tali said. "TD already likes you, can't you tell?"

She brought the horse out of his stall, putting only a halter over his head.

She started leading him out of the barn when Brent stopped her.

"Saddle?" he asked.

"Oh, no, not to go to the creek. TD would feel punished. All you have to do is hang on to me. You'll be fine. Of course, you have to hang onto the picnic hamper, too."

She laughed at the expression on his face and led TD over to some bales of hay, which she used to climb on and jump onto the horse's back. She reached out to hold the hamper while Brent tried to get on the horse.

"Hold him still!" he said, after the horse shied away several times.

"He's wondering when you're going to get on," Tali responded, laughing so hard she nearly dropped their food.

Brent finally succeeded in climbing onto the horse's back, where there was plenty of room for two people. They started out of the yard at a walk, across a field, away from the house.

His first fear of being on the horse gradually gave way to the joy he experienced in having his arms around Tali's waist, holding her tight. He imagined he could feel her heart beating wildly at his touch.

Her heart *was* beating wildly. She had no control over it. His touch did things to her that she had never felt before. Her skin felt on fire where it came into contact with his.

Other young men had been on TD behind her before. But none had affected her like this man did.

She wished their circumstances were different.

She didn't have time to worry for long, however, because they had reached the creek at a spot where a large clearing sloped gently down to the water, forming a natural beach.

Tali started laughing again when Brent nearly fell trying to get off the horse. She simply slipped a leg over, intending to slide down the horse's side.

But Brent was there. His hands held her hips and moved up above her waist as she slid slowly down to the ground.

He held her there, his hands on her breasts, his breath on her neck.

She didn't move. She couldn't move. It was heavenly being in his arms. Unconsciously, she leaned back against him as she put her hands on his arms.

His hands gently caressed her breasts as he leaned down to plant tiny, featherlike kisses on her neck.

She caught her breath, closing her eyes.

His touch was so exciting! Never had she felt this way before.

He gently turned her around. She opened her eyes, looking deep into his. She saw nothing there but love. And desire.

Definitely desire.

Her head was already tilted up, so when his lips touched hers, she simply leaned in toward him, his arms wrapping themselves around her, drawing her close.

She felt the hardness of him and her excitement mounted. She could no more have stopped his kisses and caresses than she could have stopped the creek from flowing.

She didn't want him to stop!

They were lost in time, each exploring the other's body in wonder. She was not aware of being undressed by him as she kissed his chest, his neck, his face.

They dropped to the thick, soft grass together.

They became one.

When he entered her, she gave a brief cry of pain.

They belonged together. It felt as if they were made for each other.

And when they reached their climax, both cried out. They lay together, him on top of her. She didn't want the moment to end.

His head was resting on her bare stomach, and she stroked his thick, beautiful hair.

They stayed that way for several minutes, letting their hearts quit pounding, letting their breathing become normal.

Eventually he rose up, looking at her. He reached up a hand and touched a breast. "You are so beautiful," he whispered. "Your breasts have the most beautiful shape I've ever seen."

She reached both hands up and touched his face, letting her fingers draw slowly down his cheeks.

He noticed there were tears in her eyes.

"It's okay," he reassured her. "I love you. I've loved you ever since I looked up and saw you on that horse. You're the most beautiful, most desirable woman I've ever met!"

"And I love you," she repeated. "It's just that…"

"I'm your first, aren't I?" he asked, marveling at the wonder of it. For this beautiful creature to have been untouched was beyond comprehension. And yet it was true.

"Yes, you are," she said.

"I'm glad," he said. "Now you're mine completely. Oh, I love you so much!" he cried, planting kisses on her breasts.

"Have you ever been swimming in a creek?" she asked.

"I can't say that I have," he said. "Am I about to?"

"Only if you want to," she replied. "It's quite an experience."

They jumped up and ran to the water's edge.

Although it was high summer, Brent yelled out when he plunged into the icy, cold water. This was a swift-running creek, at least in this spot, so the water stayed cold.

He came up sputtering, shivering. Once they were used to it, however, they played around in the water for a while. When they came out, they planned to let the air dry them off, but they couldn't resist one another.

They made love again, slowly, leisurely, each mounting to and exploding with passion at the same time.

Never had anything been so exciting, so satisfying, to either of them.

After enjoying the delicious meal Granny had provided, they relaxed, their backs against a tree. He reached out to take her hand, desiring always to touch her. He looked down.

"What a beautiful ring," he said, touching a diamond and ruby ring Tali wore on her right hand, pinkie finger.

She held her hand up.

"Yes, isn't it? It belonged to my grandmother, then my mother, and now it's been handed down to me. My grandmother actually wore it on her third finger, so you can imagine how tiny she was."

"Then you take after her," was his reply, giving her a look that made the blood rush to her face, making her become flushed.

His look was so full of desire that she felt an immediate response. She was actually leaning toward him, ready for his kiss, when she remembered something. She leaned back, pushing him gently away from her.

"By the way," Tali began, "I talked with Mrs. Barnett and she said you had called her about that interview. She said to call her this afternoon at three o'clock."

Brent sat up straight, looking surprised. Tali must be very close to Mrs. Barnett. He looked at his watch. It was one-thirty.

"I should hurry, then, or she'll leave her office again."

"She's not at her office."

Brent looked at her questioningly.

"She's here, in Granville, at this number. It's unlisted, so you won't find the address. She asks that you not reveal this number to anyone, okay? That's part of the deal in granting you the interview. Deal?"

As she spoke, she reached into her shirt pocket, retrieving a small, folded piece of paper.

He reached for it, but she held it away, out of his reach.

She was smiling, playing with him.

"Deal?" she asked, again.

"Deal," he said. "The number is safe with me."

He reached past her for the paper, bringing his face close to hers.

Their lips met in a slow, passionate kiss.

She was the one to push him away.

"You'll be late for your interview. We'd better pack up."

Chapter 10

They quickly gathered up everything. They touched each other as much as possible, laughing as they tickled each other. Tali whistled for TD, who was used to the call.

"May I call from your house?" Brent asked, as they trotted along on TD.

Tali stiffened. Her mind was racing. What could she do? Then she relaxed.

"Can't. Remember? No phone, it's that 'dead zone' thing for a cell phone, and Granny just doesn't want any kind of phone. We, the family, I mean, caters to her wishes," she replied.

"Oh, that's right. Then we'd really better hurry."

The number she had given him went to a small cabin

down the hill, at the back of the house, out of sight of the house and barn. It contained radio equipment and was used for the helicopter's coming and going.

It was nearly two forty-five by the time they returned to the farm.

Tali stopped at the front steps and let Brent off TD. This time, at least, he did not fall off the horse.

"I'll put TD away," she said, heading for the barn.

He barely heard her, his mind already on the coming interview, already on the questions he had written down, in case he ever did have the opportunity to speak with Mrs. Barnett.

Had he thought of everything? He wanted it to be a spectacular piece—one that all the leading magazines would want to pick up and use as a feature article. He retrieved his attaché case from the porch where he had set it when he arrived.

He looked up at Granny, grinning.

"My big moment," he said.

She smiled back at him. "Tali told me. Make the most of it, now. You may never get another chance."

"I know," he agreed.

He still had to make it into town in time.

❧❦❧

Tali heard the phone ringing before she reached the

cabin. She hurried, taking long strides, almost jogging. She had time only to put TD in his stall and brush him down before heading down here the back way. She gave Brent time to get back to town.

She cursed herself for having let the time get away from her at the creek. But who wouldn't have forgotten time in Brent's arms? Time stood still when he touched her.

He loved her! She knew that. She wanted to shout it out, tell the whole world.

But she didn't have time to think of that right now. She started running, fumbling in her shorts' pocket for her keys. She still had to unlock the door.

Brent was just ready to hang up the phone when he heard her pick it up. He had allowed it to ring over fifty times, and had decided Mrs. Barnett had changed her mind again.

"Hello? Wait!"

A breathless voice answered and Brent thought he recognized it, that it sounded familiar. Where had he heard it?

"Hello?" a voice answered again, this time different. This was Mrs. Barnett, the same one he had spoken to before. Perhaps her assistant had answered the first time.

In the cabin, Tali cursed herself. In her haste, she had answered the phone without thinking of switching on the muffler. All her lines had these same electronic devices on them.

She spent the next forty-five minutes answering Brent's

questions. For the most part, they were the normal, typical ones any reporter would ask. Some she would not answer.

Doesn't he have any imagination? she wondered.

She made a split-second decision at the end of the conversation.

"Nothing you've asked me is very exciting, Mr. Walker. I'm afraid it wouldn't be very interesting copy. Would you like an exclusive scoop?"

"Sure, of course," he replied. Now, maybe he would get somewhere. She had refused to answer any of the personal questions he had thrown at her.

"You may report that I have recently met the man of my life. I have fallen thoroughly, completely, head-over-heels in love."

"Great!" responded Brent. "Who's the lucky guy?" *What a scoop!*

"Sorry, no names," Tali said. "Just knowing there's a significant other in my life should keep some people guessing, don't you think?"

"Oh, I think, for sure," Brent said. "Better keep a look out behind you. Every reporter and his dog will be watching you now, trying to find out who this mystery man is."

"Well, I will tell you that this man loves me completely, for myself, for who I really am, not just for my money or position."

Yeah, I bet. "Great, again!" he said out loud.

The call ended with a promise by Brent to check with

her before the final copy came out. He spent several minutes after they hung up organizing his notes, which were on unnumbered pages. He neatly placed them in his attaché case.

He went as fast as he could back to the farm.

"Tali?" he asked Granny.

"Still at the barn," she replied. "Have a seat. She'll be here in a minute."

He sat down on a rocker beside her. Did she ever leave this porch or quit shelling beans?

He had his notes in his hand.

"Maybe I'd better go down there. I really can't wait to show her these, tell her about the interview with Mrs. Barnett."

"Here she comes now," Granny said, nodding toward the barn. She always sat in a chair facing both the barn and the driveway.

Brent looked that way, marveling again at Tali's beauty. And now he knew the full extent of that beauty. Every inch of her body was etched permanently into his memory. He was getting excited just watching her draw nearer and remembering their lovemaking.

"Finished?" she said, as she mounted the steps.

"Yes, and with a major scoop, too." He stood up. "Tali, do you mind if I leave for a few days? Please. Would you understand? I need to get these notes written up, okayed by Mrs. Barnett, and submitted for publication. No, I hate to leave you, especially now. How can I go? I love you so much!"

He laid the papers down and reached her in two long strides, putting his arms around her, stroking her hair.

She pushed him away, gently, and smiled up at him. "Of course I understand. Go do whatever you need to. After all, it's your job, isn't it?"

"Well, no, not exactly," he replied.

"What do you mean?" she asked.

"It's not my job."

"You're a reporter, aren't you? After all, you wanted an interview with Mrs. Barnett. Most reporters do interviews."

"Yes, they do," he agreed. "And I have submitted a few articles, through the years, to various magazines and they've been accepted for publication. But I'm not a reporter by profession, if that's what you meant."

"Then what are you?" she asked.

"Do I have to *be* anything?" he asked, smiling down at her.

Why was she being so serious?

"Most people are something," she returned. "Besides, if you aren't a reporter, why did you want to do an interview with Mrs. Barnett?"

"Why all these questions?" he countered.

"Because there has to be a reason," she insisted.

"Personal satisfaction, I guess." He shrugged. "The knowledge that I would be the first to do something. Hey, lighten up," he teased, stroking her arm. "It didn't hurt her, I assure you. Now, I do have to go. Will you remember how much I love you while I'm gone?"

"Of course," she said, reaching up, touching his face. "And I love you thoroughly, completely. I'm head-over-heels in love with you."

He frowned down at her. Those words, the way she said them. They seemed so familiar. He shook his head. Silly! They were just an expression. But it immediately began nagging at him.

Tali watched him get in his car, drive away.

Yes, she loved him. But who was he?

Granny had watched them together. Something had happened at the creek, she was sure of it. Poor Tali. Being so much in love as she obviously was with this man could mean heartaches.

And poor Brent. He would certainly have his hands full with Tali.

Granny smiled. She started humming to herself as she continued shelling beans.

Chapter 11

Tali looked up as Lily rushed in, and she blinked in surprise at her assistant. "Lily! What's wrong?"

Her usually very self-composed assistant looked flushed, nervous.

"I have just seen and talked to the most handsome, most beautiful man I have ever seen in my life. It's just too bad!" Lily exclaimed.

At least that explained the flushed cheeks.

"What's too bad?" Tali asked.

"He's on the janitorial staff, that's what's too bad!"

"So?" asked Tali, smiling. She was teasing Lily.

It was a secret with them that Lily planned to marry one of the many executives who came and went from other businesses, or even from here. She wanted someone wealthy, not a janitor.

"Actually, you never know where you might find true love," Tali responded.

Her tone held such a plaintiff note that Lily gave her a closer look.

Tali's eyes were dreamy and she seemed lost in a world of her own.

Lily remembered a certain phone call a few weeks back and her curiosity got the best of her.

"Who is he?" she asked. "You might as well tell me, you know. Is it that 'reporter' that called and you gave the interview to?"

Tali brought her glance back to her friend.

"He's not a reporter, but, yes, that's him. I'm not sure what he 'is,' though."

"Why not find out?" Lily asked, shrugging. "You have lots of people that can do that for you, you know."

"You're right," Tali agreed, with a wicked grin. "Let's find out just who, or what, this Mr. Brent Walker is!"

❧❧

While Brent slowly and deliberately worked on the baseboards along the hall, he kept an eye on the office door.

Earlier an older woman had gone in, then the assistant. Could the older woman have been Mrs. Barnett? She hadn't come out yet, but she could just be another assistant.

He had thought of the possibility of there being another door to the office, but he hoped not.

But the assistant! Now, there was an idea. He could tell she was attracted to him, simply by the way she blushed and stammered when she tripped over him and he raised up. He was used to having this effect on women. There was just one now, of course, that he wanted to have this effect on, and did. He thought of Tali, and their lovemaking, and wanted to be with her so much. But he also wanted to find out about Mrs. Barnett. He almost put his equipment away and headed for Granville, but contained himself. He missed Tali so much! His desire for her was so great he was surprised at himself. He had been with lots of women, but no one had aroused such excitement, so many feelings within him.

Brent's patience paid off. In his work kit, he had a camera in a bag, disguised as equipment. When he saw the young assistant go in, he positioned the bag so that the camera faced the door. He held the remote control in his hand. This old VCR recorder was all he could find on such short notice when he decided to try to take these sneak photos. He had thought many times of throwing it away, because people were switching over to other recorders and DVD machines. But now he was glad he had tossed it up on the top shelf of his closet. It worked out perfectly for this purpose.

Also, since he knew there was a VCR machine at Granny's, he planned to go there and share this tape with

Tali. They could watch it together and she would verify that he had caught Mrs. Barnett on tape.

Presently, the door opened and the older lady stepped out. At the same time, a man had been coming down the hall, and he was a few feet from the door when the woman stepped out.

Almost colliding, they looked at each other.

Brent noticed the surprised look on the man's face, which quickly changed to pleasure. He reached out and hugged the woman and she returned the embrace. Her face was only partially toward Brent, and her hair hid most of her face. He kept the camcorder going, however, as the two talked and laughed.

He could not make out the words they were saying, but once the woman laughed and Brent stopped cold in his tracks. The woman's laughter sounded so much like Tali's that he immediately pictured her in front of him, laughing up at him, her eyes sparkling.

The moment passed, though, so Brent knew he had just imagined the laugh being so much like hers. How he missed her! And, now, with this video, he could go back to Granville, to see Tali. He was sure there would be something in the video he could use as a still and submit with his article.

The two of them started up the hall the other way, still chatting as old friends.

Could this man be the mystery lover?

In front of the elevators, they reached out, touched

hands, then leaned forward for a goodbye kiss, on the lips.

That was good. He hoped it wasn't too far away from the video camera to get a good shot. As soon as the elevator doors closed on the woman, and the man started toward him again, he began to put his work equipment away.

As usual, the man simply walked past him, paying no attention to one of the maintenance staff in overalls.

Chapter 12

"Mrs. Barnett's office," Lily said into the phone in her most professional voice. "Lily speaking."

"Lily! What a beautiful name!" a voice breathed, and Lily felt her heart skip a beat. She knew that voice!

No matter how hard she had tried, she had been unable to forget that voice, or the gorgeous man it belonged to. Even if he were just a maintenance worker, she had found herself watching for him and looking down halls, hoping to get another look at him. If she saw him, she would think of some excuse to talk to him. But for a week now, she had not seen him.

She had even made excuses to go on trips to other floors. No luck.

And now here he was, phoning her.

"This is your friendly maintenance man. Do you remember tripping over me last week?"

Do I? "Oh, you're the one painting the baseboards?" she asked, in what she hoped was a casual, indifferent tone.

But he wasn't fooled. He chuckled. "The same. I'm so glad you remember."

"How did you know my name?" Lily asked.

"Oh, we men always have ways of getting the names of pretty women we meet, or get run over by, whichever."

His voice still held an amused tone.

"And what can I help you with, Mr…" she asked, leaving the question open, obviously waiting for his name.

"Call me Michael," Brent responded, in the appropriate time. He hadn't expected to be asked, so he used the first name that came to mind. "And you can help me by rescuing me from a lonely, boring evening tonight. Will you have dinner with me tonight?"

"Why tonight?" she asked.

"Why not?" was his response.

He wasn't used to being questioned like this. The only one doing that lately was Tali. Most women eagerly accepted his invitations.

"I mean, we met, or rather, I fell over you, a week ago. Why wait until now to ask me out? Were you booked up until now or did someone just call and cancel?"

No matter how impressed she had been by his good

looks and wonderfully sexy voice, she was simply not going to be that easy!

Has this women been taking lessons on being difficult from her boss or does this just rub off by association? Brent wondered. "I had some personal, some family business to take care of. I haven't even been to work there. Had to take some time off."

She *had* noticed that.

"But I'm back in the city now. I haven't been able to get you off my mind. So how about dinner?"

"Sure, I'm free tonight. But I live in this building, and it gets locked at a certain time. Can you meet me at the main entrance?"

"Of course. Eightish?" he agreed.

"I'll be here."

"Until then," he said, softly into the phone, again sending goose pimples down her arms.

Why did this man affect her so? "Yes," she breathed in response. She placed the phone gently in its cradle.

On the other end of the line, Brent sat for a minute by the phone, reflecting on this last move of his. Did he feel bad about using Lily this way? No, he decided. If they both had fun and enjoyed each other's company, that was reason enough to have dinner and get better acquainted. If he could bring her a few minutes pleasure, help her to enjoy her life more, then it didn't make any difference what his motives were.

Most of his business associates would agree that his ends always justified the means. There would be a few, however, who thought his methods of dealing with things somewhat unorthodox.

He would take this opportunity to be with Lily and find out as much as he could about Mrs. Barnett. Tomorrow he would go to Granville and view the tape with Granny and Tali.

Lily *was* pretty. He had to give her that. She was standing inside the outer glass door, waiting for him. When he approached, she waved to the man behind the security desk, who got up and locked the door behind her as she stepped out onto the sidewalk.

She drew in her breath.

In his Armani suit, he was so beautiful. He carried himself so well, that it seemed as if the suit had been made just for him. He could have been born into it. But how could he afford such clothes on the salary he was bound to be making?

"Two jobs," he said, as if he could read her thoughts. "And a brother-in-law in the business."

He laughed, and she laughed, too.

It felt so easy, so good, being with him.

She was so fascinated by the place they went that she didn't mind his questions about her over dinner. She answered questions about her job, Tali—although he thought of her boss as Mrs. Barnett—and her living arrangements.

He answered her questions openly, so she thought they were just getting to know each other better. And that suited her just fine!

He was so easy to talk to and so handsome!

After dinner, they walked a while, arm in arm. When they reached the office building, she found herself inviting him up to her apartment, which was on the penthouse level. He gladly accepted.

This was the opportunity he had been waiting for. He had not expected it on the first evening. He had been prepared to date her for several weeks, or as long as it took, to get upstairs, near Mrs. Barnett's living quarters.

He pretended interest in such an unusual arrangement as living in the same place you worked, right next to the boss.

When the elevator doors opened on the top floor, or actually the next to the top floor, he immediately took in every detail, the arrangement of every door in the short hallway.

Lily pointed to Margaret's door. "And T—Margaret lives there."

"Who?" he asked.

"Margaret. Mrs. Barnett. I started to call her by her nickname, which would not have meant anything to you."

"Which is…" he coaxed.

But Lily's attention was at the door, as she fumbled with her keys. She was extremely nervous. She had never invited a man to her apartment on the first date before. She wasn't sure what she expected, or wanted, from him. Or, on the other hand, what he expected.

As she opened the door, she glanced back at him. He was staring at Tali's door.

"Michael?" she invited, holding the door open.

He looked back at her, a smile on his face. He stepped through the door to her apartment, which he quickly ascertained was really a townhouse. So, that's why the elevator didn't go completely to the top floor.

"What a place!" he commented.

And it was.

As you walked in, two sofas were set at right angles to each other, which provided a cozy-looking, inviting spot for reading, watching television, or just conversing with guests. Built-in shelves on either side of the room gave it the added feeling of a library. Most of the shelves were filled with books, interspersed with knick-knacks and photos in frames.

The area opened to the dining area, and a wood-and-tile table with Windsor-style chairs gave it a formal, yet lived-in look. On one wall, there was a formal chest with a mirror about it, giving the illusion of added space and light to the room. The ceramic tiles on the table were of a grape design, which accentuated the deep green and scarlet of the living area. To accent the table, a floor lamp was placed near it, opposite a fireplace. He wondered how many people she entertained at one time. The lamp was on, providing an added glow to the design of the table. He was sure this was a planned effect and the lamp stayed on most of the time.

The kitchen had a curved counter on the dining room side. See-through cabinets let light in and further gave the feeling of space.

The living room and dining room both shared a cathedral ceiling, revealing beams, which added to the character of the place. Natural light flowing through a sky light revealed the inner beauty of the hardwood beams.

Lily loved light. On one wall, right angles to the shelves, another large mirror, as a decorating accent, reflected the architectural style of the overhead beams.

Brent let out a long, low whistle.

"You like?" Lily asked.

"I sure do. It reminds me of—" Brent didn't finish. He had involuntarily started to say that it reminded him of Tali, but stopped himself in time. He had learned long ago that you don't mention one lady while in the company of another.

"It reminds you of what?" she asked.

"Just some of the photos I've seen in house furnishing magazines. Have you ever had it photographed for one?"

She was flattered, as was his intention. He had thought fast on that one!

"Not that I know of. Please, take a look upstairs," she said, gesturing toward the staircase.

"Is that an invitation?" he asked with a wicked grin.

Lily blushed, then quickly regained her composure. "Maybe."

He smiled at her, apparently enjoying her confusion. This man had such an animal magnetism about him and he obviously knew the effect he had on women.

He started up the stairs. "Coming?" he asked, looking down at her, enjoying the position it put him in.

She had to look up at him. "You go on," she said. "I'll get us some coffee."

She made a point of looking directly up at his face, studiously avoiding any other areas of his body.

He laughed softly, starting to go up again.

The main bedroom was tastefully done, by Lily, he assumed, as he had expected. The walls were a robin's-egg blue, but a bright array of colors added contrast. An upholstered headboard was raised above the bed and attached to the wall. Above that, four watercolors of flowers were symmetrically arranged. Plantation shutters on the windows on each side of the bed kept the space open and bright.

Another mirror decorated one wall. It was made from an old window frame. It added an even sunnier look to the room.

The whole apartment reminded him of Tali. He had no idea why.

Lily appeared in the doorway.

"You have excellent taste," he said. "I love the whole apartment."

"Thanks. My boss and I both planned and decorated it. Hers is very similar to this. We grew up together, so we always had the same tastes, it seemed."

Lily continued to rattle on about the apartment, but Brent's thoughts locked on her one statement about her boss. How could they grow up together yet be so far apart in age? Mrs. Barnett had gray hair and looked old enough, at least from the back and side, to be Lily's mother. He brought his attention back to Lily, who was pointing out a painting to him. His eye caught the scene of a farmhouse, barn, trees, but his thoughts were still far away.

"…our hometown. He was a local artist," she concluded. She looked at Brent, expecting an answer.

He looked straight at her, smiling, causing her to catch her breath.

"How about that coffee?" he asked, taking her elbow, gently turning her toward the stairs. He followed her down.

He had seen enough to know how Mrs. Barnett's apartment was also laid out. All he needed was a key to the elevator to get to this level.

His opportunity came a short time later when Lily went to another room. Her phone rang and she excused herself to go talk on the phone.

Brent quickly took the elevator key off her ring. Quickly taking a piece of clay in a plastic container out of his jacket pocket, he pushed just hard enough with the key to make an impression. He closed the lid. He had the plastic case in his pocket and key back on her ring while she was still on the phone. He shook his head. Why had this thing with Mrs. Barnett become such an obsession with him that he was stooping so low as to steal keys? But he couldn't seem to stop himself. He had to see in her apartment. He had his jacket on and was by the door when Lily returned.

She looked disappointed, but brightened considerably when he made another date with her. He would see her tomorrow night.

❧❧❧

Brent found himself on the turnpike heading south without consciously being aware that he had come this way. But he knew where he was headed!

Granville and Tali.

Chapter 13

s Brent neared Granville, he heard the familiar "chop-chop" of helicopter blades overhead. It seemed to go directly over him and then veered off toward Granville.

On an impulse, Brent braked quickly and turned down the same dirt, bumpy road he had first traveled on when he came to Granville. This time, instead of creeping along, he kept a steady pace, in spite of the bouncing around. He would need an alignment for sure after this and probably another new tire. Or all of them.

But he could see the chopper in the sky in front of him, and he didn't want to lose it.

Suddenly, the chopper dipped, going out of sight below the trees. Where could it have gone? That was flat land up there. In fact, he had to be getting close to Tali's farmhouse.

Before he could do any more speculating, the chopper rose again in the sky, vertically, and came back toward him. It seemed as if it had delivered its passengers and/or cargo.

But where had it landed? It had to be close, and the distance made it exactly at Tali's.

Well, he was going there, anyway, so he could ask about it, after he showed them the video.

Since there had to be lots of roads around Granville that he had not yet explored, he decided to find another one that led to the farmhouse. And there had to be a road that led to Mrs. Barnett's.

His best bet was probably the old man at the service station where he had stopped when he was first looking for Granville. If anyone would know, surely he would.

When he pulled into the old service station, it seemed as if nothing had changed in the past few weeks.

The old man was sitting in the same place. Had he even moved?

"Back again, huh?" he asked as Brent approached him.

"You remember me?"

"Don't get too many strangers around here. Sure, I remember you. Found Granville yet?"

"Yes, finally," Brent replied. "Now can you tell me if there are any other ways into Granville? I took a couple of roads out of town, but just seemed to circle around and come back to the same spot."

The old man nodded. "Yep, it can happen if you don't know your way around. There are several ways into town. Last time you wanted the closest, that's what I gave you. Which way you want now?"

"Any other, really," Brent replied.

The man grinned. "Okay, let me think." He pushed back his cap and scratched his head while he held onto the cap. "Go down past the road you took last time," he began, pointing that way. "'Bout a quarter of a mile past there is another road. Winds around a bit but you'll eventually come to Granville. Real scenic, it is."

The "eventually" was what made Brent wonder about it. He started to ask about any others when the old man spoke again.

"Goes past the old LeDieux plantation, then watch out. Washed out in a couple of places several years back. Past the washouts, there's three roads you can take. Take the left-hand one, get you into Granville."

"The LeDieux plantation?" Brent asked. That sounded interesting. He hadn't yet seen a home large enough to be considered a plantation.

"Yep. The LeDieux family's owned it since before the War."

Somehow, Brent knew the old man meant the Civil War. He would not have been able to explain how he knew, he just did. Time seemed to stand still in this place.

"'Course, some newcomers call it the Old Barnett place

but us old-timers know it as the LeDieux plantation. Was LeDieux before Claire LeDieux married Barnett. Don't that still make it LeDieux?"

The old man was on a roll. Brent wasn't sure if he really expected an answer or not. He didn't care. When he heard the name Barnett, he knew he was home free. That's the road he wanted.

"Thank you, sir," he began, holding out his hand to shake the old man's.

The man took it but stopped Brent. "Can't go down there in that," he said, pointing to the BMW. "Bottom out."

"Bottom out?" Brent asked. What did he mean?

"Yep, there's some pretty big rocks on that road, I'm told, especially where it washed out. Better take a four-wheel drive."

"Is there a car rental place near?" Brent asked.

That produced a large guffaw from the old man. "Nope, but you can take Ole Blue there, if you want to. He'll hold up. Just go slow."

Brent looked over to where the old man was pointing. There sat an old—*very old,* Brent thought—faded blue Ford pickup. Vintage '50s, he figured. Maybe early '60s, but no later. Could he even drive such a thing?

The old man was digging into his pockets of his overalls for his keys. He held them out to Brent.

"You'd trust me with your pickup?"

"Sure," the old man agreed. "You'll be leaving that

here, won't you?" he asked, pointing to the BMW. "Who'd lose if you don't come back?"

His big grin revealed missing teeth. But the grin was genuine. He thought it was funny.

"You're right, of course."

"He's full. Just enjoy."

The old man still thought it was funny. He probably thought it was funny that a city slicker would want to use the pickup.

The only reason Brent would, of course, was that it would get him to Mrs. Barnett's house. *Excuse me— plantation.*

Chapter 14

The old pickup really wasn't that bad to drive. It started right up and handled easily. The old man certainly kept it in tiptop shape.

It took Brent quite a while of bouncing over a rougher road than the first one old Burt had sent him down before he came to a high wrought iron fence. No house was in sight but he bet it was the beginning of someone's property. Someone with enough money to put this entire fence in place. The fence was obviously old, in an architectural style not seen for at least a hundred years. But it was in excellent repair.

Another half mile brought him to an elaborate iron gate. He stopped the pickup and got out. The gate was locked, as he expected it to be. He stood there looking in.

The scene was incredible, breathtaking in its beauty. Tall, large stately pines lined a long driveway up to what he knew was an antebellum mansion. What he could see of the home revealed four large columns supporting a two-story house with a balcony across the second story.

The pines prevented a full view of the house. They were the type of pines that grew very wide with large "skirts" around the bottom of the trunk. The lower branches even brushed the ground. He thought a child could part those branches and have enough room within them to make a playhouse around the trunk of the tree. He did not know the scientific or even common name of these pines. He only saw their majestic beauty and was in awe of them.

A one-lane drive went to the house and he could picture the circular drive in front of it. He could imagine horses pulling beautiful carriages containing just as beautiful young ladies in wonderful ball gowns. He could see the carriages stopping at the front of the house and butlers helping these young ladies down out of the carriages.

He supposed what he was picturing was something out of *Gone with the Wind,* but he could see that as being a true portrayal of what happened at these stately homes before the Civil War.

The very air around the place produced a peaceful languor within him. He didn't want to move.

He was so caught up in his dreams that he had not heard anyone approach.

"Found it, did you?" a voice asked, interrupting his thoughts.

He jumped, turning around.

A man atop a wagon was stopped there in the lane. It was pulled by a Clydesdale. How could he have approached without Brent hearing it? But he had.

Brent recognized one of the men from the boarding house.

"Accidentally, I assure you."

The man nodded toward the pickup. "Driving Burt's truck, ain't you?"

"Does better on these roads than mine," Brent agreed, grinning.

"You ain't wrong there," the man agreed.

"This is a beautiful place," Brent said, looking back again at the house.

"Sure is."

"Does anyone live here now?" Brent asked.

"Sure. Of course."

The man seemed surprised by such a question.

"It just seems so…deserted…for some reason," Brent said by way of explanation.

"People just don't use the road anymore, that's all. Got pretty washed out several years back. Granny LeDieux still lives here, though, and a companion. Granny doesn't get out much but her companion comes and goes."

"The helicopter!" Brent exclaimed.

"Of course. Surely you've seen it. Goes over town quite a bit."

"Yes, I've seen it. I wondered where it landed."

"Open field behind the house. But don't get any more or better ideas about being able to get to the house. That gate there stays locked and you can't get to the back of the house. Not by land, I mean. Only by helicopter. Wouldn't try it, though. Wouldn't be welcome, if you know what I mean."

"I know what you mean," Brent agreed. Hadn't he already met such resistance, such reluctance on the part of everyone in town to tell him how to get here.

"Burt tell you about this place?" the man asked quietly.

Brent sensed trouble for the old man at the service station and wasn't willing to do that to him. "No. I just asked him about some other roads into town and he told me if I took some of them, I'd need his pickup. Actually, he steered me the other way. I had seen this one from the highway and decided to take it. I'm glad I had the pickup."

The old man nodded, satisfied. If Brent had found the place on his own, that was okay. But if Burt had told him how to get here, that was another matter altogether.

"After seeing this place I can't blame anyone for wanting to protect the privacy and serenity of it."

"Yep, Granny and her companion. She doesn't want Granny bothered by a bunch of reporters. Or anyone, for that matter."

"I know what you mean," Brent agreed again. "It's so quiet here. Dogs?" he asked.

The man laughed. "Just a lickin-pot hound. Wouldn't hurt the fleas on his own back. And he's not here half the time."

"I've seen enough. See you later, okay?" Brent walked to the pickup.

The man moved his horse and wagon into the driveway space in front of the gate so that Brent could go on down the lane.

Brent would go on around to town and back to pick up his own car. He had seen enough. He wasn't quite sure yet what he would do with what he had learned today.

He did know, though, that he wanted to see Tali.

∽∾∽

As Brent pulled to a stop in front of the farmhouse, Tali flew out the front door and into his arms, nearly causing him to lose his balance.

He held her close and then raised her face to meet his lips in a long, passionate kiss. How good it felt to be loved!

Tali pushed him away, suddenly embarrassed at her brazen display of emotions. She had always been very self-controlled. But she had never met anyone like him before. It seemed impossible to control her thoughts and actions around him.

But he loved her, and that's all that mattered!

Chapter 15

Did you hear that?" Tali exclaimed, standing up. Both Brent and Granny looked up at her, wondering what she was talking about, momentarily ignoring the video tape, which continued to run.

"What? Hear what?" Brent repeated, his eyes never leaving Tali's face.

"Turn it off a minute. Hurry!" she said, gesturing toward the TV.

Brent pushed the "stop" button on the remote control without hesitating. He looked at her questioningly.

"We have to check on TD," she said. "Come with me?"

"What did you hear?" he asked.

"TD, and he never nickers like that unless something's wrong, maybe something or somebody in the barn. Let's go, okay?"

"Sure," Brent agreed, rising from his chair.

It was late afternoon, the shadows were long, and he did not want her going to the barn by herself, although he felt that was probably foolish of himself. Obviously, she'd been going to the barn to check on the horse at all hours of the day and night, long before they met. However, as long as he was around, he would not let her go alone.

They had reached the porch when Tali grabbed his arm to stop him.

"Flashlight," she said. "Wait here."

She was gone back inside before he could respond. He stayed still, enjoying a cool breeze that rippled through the giant oaks covering the front yard, oaks that spread their huge branches toward each other, touching as if caressing. He strained to hear any other noises from the direction of the barn. He didn't hear anything, but he knew Tali was more attune to listening for the horse than he was. She would be aware of any unusual sounds around this place.

It seemed to take her several minutes to get a flashlight, but he was patient. He would wait on this woman forever. Just thinking of her now made him warm, wishing he had his arms around her and his lips on hers. He could feel his body inside hers and his desire started to mount.

Then she was back.

"Sorry. It wasn't in its usual place," she began, then stopped.

The look he was giving her sent quivers up and down

her back. The desire was clear and apparent in his eyes, and she felt her own desire respond to him. But this was not the time or place. She stepped forward and put her arm through his, turning him to descend the steps of the porch.

Tali was shocked at what she just saw. Her first reaction was to stop the tape however she could. How did he get this tape? Who made it for him? Lily had mentioned the new janitor on their floor at the office, how handsome he was. Could he have made the tape? Tali just couldn't picture anyone on her staff of loyal employees who would do such a thing. They had all sworn statements to protect her identity.

She was furious and would certainly find out who took this. But, how could she ask Brent about it, as Tali, without giving herself away to him as Mrs. Barnett?

It had only taken her a few seconds of watching the tape to recognize the hallway outside her office door at the corporate building. She had made an instant decision to divert him and get Granny to hide the tape.

Checking on TD was the first thing that had come to mind and, after that, she could say a neighbor had dropped by to borrow some tapes, taking his tape by mistake. TD's nickering could come from the fact that the neighbors had ridden horses up to the back of the house, and he had sensed them. Horses always responded that way to the presence of other horses. Yes, they could pull that story off.

She hid her anger the best she could. She would not let

him see her reaction right now. By the time they returned to the house, Granny would have taken care of it, somehow.

They walked in silence to the barn. Tali did not know how to respond to him just now. Once inside the door, however, in the dark interior, when they turned to face one another, she fell into his arms. In spite of herself, she could not resist him.

They needed no words.

He tenderly kissed her mouth then her face. His tongue explored her neck as she leaned against him, her head back. If he had not been holding her, she would have fallen. She clung to him, his powerful arms pulling her close, her fingernails digging into the hard muscles of his back.

When he led her to a clear stall, she did not protest as he removed a blanket from the dividing panel, spread it out, and placed it on the floor.

On their knees, they caressed. Without even knowing when and how, their clothes were off, their bodies coming together as they lay on the blanket.

When he entered her, she gasped with a pleasure she did not know could be duplicated. Yet, it wasn't a duplicate of the time at the creek, the first time they made love. This time was even more passionate, more pleasurable.

Their bodies moved in perfect unison, perfect harmony. As their passion mounted, their release came at the same time, bringing with it such pleasure that they both cried out, unable to stop the flow of emotional wave after wave.

Afterward, they lay together, body to body, as their breathing returned to normal.

"I have never felt like this before," Brent whispered in her ear, when he was able to talk again. "You are so beautiful."

"I love you," Tali responded, simply. She could think of nothing else. "You make me feel so beautiful, so perfect." She turned to look at him, their faces only inches apart, and smiled. "You make me glad I'm a woman."

"Oh, I'm definitely glad you're a woman," he returned, gently kissing her.

They heard a soft nicker from TD's stall.

Tali laughed softly. "I wonder what he thinks this is."

"Oh, I wouldn't be surprised if he knows," Brent answered, sounding serious.

"Do you really think so?" she asked, also serious.

Brent laughed. "Who knows? But I wouldn't be surprised. Looks like he's okay, though."

"Oh!" Tali exclaimed, rising and looking around for her clothes. "We forgot."

"We had more important things to do," Brent said.

He leaned on one elbow, his hand on his head, watching her put on her clothes. He didn't want to hurry. He cherished the moments following lovemaking with her and enjoyed just being in her company almost as much.

"Coming?" Tali asked.

"Only if I have to," he said.

She gave him a look.

"Okay, I have to," he said, smiling.

He took his time dressing, though, watching her as she stroked TD, talking to the horse as if he understood what she was saying. But maybe the horse did understand more than humans realized.

Brent walked over to them, reaching up to pick small bits of hay out of Tali's hair.

She smiled at him.

"Just removing the evidence," he said, returning the smile.

"Oh, you," she said, blushing, turning back to the horse to hide it.

"What do you think disturbed him?" he asked.

"Oh, there could have been a number of things," she began. "Sometimes maybe a snake, a rabbit, or just his imagination."

She had not been prepared, though, for the look of desire and passion in his eyes when she returned to the front porch from quickly asking Granny to help her. She was certainly not ready for the instant response she felt in her own body to his mood.

Tali wasn't ready yet to reveal her other self to Brent. She still felt there was more to him than she knew and her men had not reported back to her yet. Until then, she wanted to keep her real identify a secret.

And who knew what was on that tape? He obviously

hadn't recognized her in her "older woman" disguise, but he had said that a man he had hired had taken some of the tape. Had he lied about this?

Knowing that someone had been able to record her in her own building made her decide to "beef up" the security, especially on her floor and the floor above and below it. She would also put an extra guard on her own apartment, even though it was a secure elevator. She did not want anyone to be able to get that close to her private apartment, whether she was there or not.

She did not underestimate Brent's intelligence. It would not take him a second to put things together—little things, that, when taken separately, could be innocent happenings. But in light of the true facts, they would fit together perfectly.

Brent reached up to stroke TD, and the horse nickered softly in response, the same nicker he gave Tali.

She felt a sudden tug of something.

Jealousy? Pique that her horse held affection for this man as well as for herself? Maybe TD just smelled her on Brent, and so accepted him as a friend.

"He sure doesn't seem as if he's bothered about anything," Brent said, still stroking him.

"No, he doesn't," she admitted, "but let's look around, anyway."

They searched the barn and pastures, but found nothing. Finally, Tali figured enough time had gone by that her plan would work. They gave TD a few more pats before turning and slowly walking back to the house.

Their passion spent, they simply enjoyed the touch of their arms around each other, his around her shoulders and hers around his slim waist. It didn't pay to move too fast in the heat, anyway. The session in the barn had proved that!

"How about some lemonade?" she asked, as they climbed the steps to the front porch.

"I'd rather have you," he whispered in her ear.

She turned and gave him a stern look, telling him to be quiet, but her smile belied her apparent anger. She didn't pretend that Granny was not aware of what was going on. Her granny was plenty sharp.

They sat at the kitchen table as Granny poured lemonade from a huge pitcher on the cabinet. Granny joined them.

They laughed and enjoyed their cold drinks.

"Time to watch that video," Brent said, carrying his glass to the counter to pour himself another lemonade.

He did not see Tali and Granny exchange glances or Granny's almost imperceptible nod. Tali relaxed. Granny had taken care of everything.

As Tali and Brent went toward the family room, Granny stayed to clean the glasses.

They weren't settled for even a minute when Brent looked at Tali and exclaimed, "What's wrong with this remote?"

She stared back at him, surprised, and shrugged. "It

was working earlier. Do batteries go dead that quickly, just from one time to another?"

"I guess it's possible," Brent responded, sounding puzzled. He got up and walked to the VCR, then pushed the eject button. Nothing came out. He pushed it again.

"The tape's gone!" he exclaimed.

"Oh, no!" Granny said, from the doorway between the kitchen and the family room. "He couldn't have."

"Who couldn't have what?" Tali asked, playing along.

"Jess and Little Jess showed up at the back door just a minute after you two walked out the front. Little Jess said you told him a while back he could come borrow tapes any time he wanted."

Tali nodded.

Brent looked grim. "And he took the one out of the machine. I knew it. I should have changed the label."

"Why? What was on it?" Tali asked. She had not paid attention to the tape earlier.

"*Beetlejuice*," he said, looking sheepish.

"*Beetlejuice*?" Tali repeated, incredulously. She broke out laughing. She just couldn't help it. "Little Jess is really going to get a surprise, isn't he?"

"But how did they get here?" Brent asked. "We were out back, but on the side of the driveway. We would have heard a car come up."

"First thing I knew, there they were at the side door. Rode over," Granny said.

"Rode over?" Brent repeated. "You mean, like, on horses?"

"Yep. Said the gate was open." Granny looked over at Tali. "That's unusual, but it could happen, I suppose."

"Anything's possible," Tali replied. "And that would explain why TD whinnied. But he would have stopped, because he knows those horses."

"What are we going to do about getting that tape back?" Brent asked.

"Right now?" Tali reached out and pulled him up. "Nothing. Let's go to the county fair. We can watch the tape later. No hurry, right?"

"County fair?"

"Yes. Ever been to one before, city slicker?" Her tone was teasing.

"No, I can't say I have. What's at a county fair?"

"Oh, a little of everything," she said. "Granny even has some preserves and a quilt entered this year."

"Entered?" he asked.

"Yes, anyone who wants to can enter different items in different categories to be judged. They give blue, red, white ribbons. Granny usually gets a couple of blue, at least."

"Really?" he asked, looking over at Granny.

"Ain't nothing," Granny responded, trying to appear modest.

But Brent could tell she was very proud of the work she did and wanted it to be on display for everyone to see.

"Well, what are we waiting for?" he asked. "Let's go to my very first county fair."

"Oh, you'll love it. Coming, Granny?"

"Sure, child, you know I don't miss a chance to go, even early like this. I haven't seen the animal barns yet."

"Animal barns?" Brent mouthed silently, looking over quizzically at Tali.

His eyes were so large, she couldn't help laughing at him again. "You'll see. Today will be a day of surprises. Let's take the pickup."

"What pickup?" he asked.

What was this? He was always finding out surprising things about her. Yet, come to think of it, he had only seen her on TD. She must have a vehicle somewhere. There was a large area with a big door attached to the barn. He hadn't tried to go in there earlier. That must be what she used for a garage.

It was. Tali told him to wait there, she would bring the pickup around.

He wasn't surprised when she pulled around the house in a late model Dodge Ram, full-size. It was burgundy, with leather seats. Whatever she did or the income she had, she always had the best.

She asked him to drive.

As they rode along toward town, Tali wondered again who he was and where he was from, if he had never attended a county fair. County fairs were as American as apple pie. She smiled to herself at her own pun. Granny had entered an apple pie.

Brent knew he could make another tape. This time, he would hire someone else to do it, probably one of the maintenance staff. He would make someone an offer he couldn't refuse.

Chapter 16

Brent's first shock came when they got caught up in a long line of cars headed toward a large field. They were directed to turn into the field by a man signaling with a flashlight, although it wasn't quite dark yet. When they turned into the field, another man motioned them toward a certain row of cars, which Brent obediently followed. When he came to a stop at the end of the row, another car pulled in beside him immediately. The row was quickly filling up.

Brent turned off the engine and leaned back on the door, looking straight at Tali. She burst out laughing again at the expression on his face.

"We're parked in a field," he said in disbelief. "In a field!"

Tali was still laughing and Granny couldn't help smiling.

"I've never parked in a field in my life," he said, looking around.

He watched other cars come in the same way they had. Families with young children piled out of all sorts of vehicles, laughing, excited about the fair, anticipating what a good time they were going to have. They seemed to accept the fact that this parking in the field was the norm.

Tali had settled down a bit, but she was wiping her eyes with a Kleenex. "And, please, watch where you step when you get out," she said.

Brent's head jerked around, his eyes huge in his face.

"Cows," she said simply.

Brent could not control the expression on his face, an expression that again sent Tali into howls of laughter. She opened her door to get out, signaling for him to follow suit.

"You are presently in Farmer Brown's field, freshly mowed and baled last week so it would be available for parking this week for the fair. He always lets us park here. Free, of course," she added. "But he does let his cows graze here, also."

"You mean there really is a Farmer Brown?" he asked. At first, he thought she was joking.

"Really," she said. "Elias Brown. Nice man. Maybe we'll see him here. This is the first day of the fair. If he's here, I'll introduce you."

Granny was already out and went on her own way. She knew where to find her friends. They would spend some time looking at—and being critical of—all the sewing, needlepoint, quilting, and other arts and crafts that had been entered. Granny herself would judge many categories of crafts that she had nothing entered in. Her opinion was always valued and highly sought after, and had been for many years.

Brent looked around on the ground before he put even one foot out. Tali came around the pickup, taking his hand in hers as he slowly emerged from the vehicle.

He was still scanning the ground. The grass was several inches high, but they seemed to have parked in a cleared, level field.

"County" was the operative word here. The place was packed. People were walking to the entrance gate from all over the parking lot—field—parking field. He was sure getting some good stories to tell his friends about the challenge he had chosen for The Game this year.

"It's not really that bad," Tali said. "Come on. You'll enjoy it."

"Promise?" he asked, still not sure.

"Promise," Tali said firmly.

As they walked toward the entrance to the fairgrounds, many people, couples, and families alike greeted Tali. Brent watched the Ferris Wheel, the Hammer, and other rides as they shot up into the sky and then plummeted back down.

But he didn't miss the fact that so many people knew and acknowledged Tali.

She had a smile and greeting for everyone.

"Miss Tali, Miss Tali!" came one excited cry.

Tali stopped as a young boy caught up with them.

"Look!" he said, as he proudly held up a large bullfrog for her to see.

Brent took an involuntarily step backward, out of sheer surprise.

Tali, however, seemed undaunted. She leaned down and touched the animal.

"Boy, that's a big one, Billy Joe," she said. "Where did you find him?"

"Jackson's pond, fishing yesterday. He's some frog, huh?"

Tali smiled. "Sure is."

"Gotta go," Billy Joe said, as he turned to run and join his family.

"You actually touched that thing," Brent said.

"Of course, I suppose you think I'll get warts or something, right?"

"Well..." Brent said, his voice trailing off, not sure what he wanted to believe.

He had heard that old wives' tale. He had also figured this excursion might be a culture shock, but he had not been prepared to touch all the critters he might see, or to have Tali touch them, either. Most of the women he had dated would have been appalled even at the thought of being near a frog like that.

Tali just laughed, causing him to relax and laugh, too. It was either laugh or cry, so he chose the laughter. He decided to relax and enjoy himself, no matter what came their way.

But he always wanted to laugh when he was with Tali, no matter where they were. She just had that kind of effect on him. His life had been one of stress, trying to impress people. But he had no such pressure with Tali. His love for her was so great that sometimes he wasn't sure he could contain it—he felt it would explode out of him.

Where pride had been such a factor when dealing with other women, he had no pride where Tali was concerned.

It seemed she was always so full of surprises. Most of the other women he knew held no more interest for him. They all seemed to be and act the same. Tali was different.

They joined the line at the entrance. Brent was surprised and glad to pay the three dollars per ticket the young lady at the booth asked for. When you were used to paying the price for Broadway or Met tickets, this came as a welcome surprise.

There were so many sights and sounds that he, at first, only had an impression of noise. Slowly he started distinguishing certain sounds and identifying what they were. He heard, first of all, the delighted squeals of girls, boys, and even adults as they soared into the air and plummeted toward the ground at lightning speeds, all aboard various rides.

Some rides went around and around in a swirl of color and noise.

Concentrating on only one particular ride, Brent saw the expressions on faces as not that of joy, but often as fear or even pain. Some of the rides seemed to cause the riders to transcend the state of pleasure, plunging the joyrider into some other state. Grimaces of all sorts contorted the faces of boys and girls, men and women alike.

Yet, as incredible as it seemed, when the rides stopped and the people emerged from their seats or positions on the rides, they were smiling, laughing. Often, they would get back into line to enjoy the same ride again. This was especially true of the children and teenagers. It seemed they could never get enough.

"Let's go through the dairy barn, first, then the beef," she said, putting her arm through his, starting toward the barns. "Then we'll decide what rides we want to go on."

Brent didn't move, causing Tali to come to a quick halt. She looked at him.

"The what?" he asked.

He had such a comical, quizzical look on his face that she just had to laugh.

"The dairy barn is the building where they display the dairy cattle," she said, still laughing.

"Why do they want to do that?" he asked, puzzled.

"To be judged, of course," she responded.

"Judged? Judged for what? A cow's a cow, isn't it?"

She just smiled, shaking her head. "Now, that's a true city slicker talking."

"Well," he responded drily. "I'll have to admit I haven't seen too many cows—dairy ones, did you say?—lately on the streets of Paris, London, or New York City."

"Oh, so you're a frequent traveler to those cities, are you?" she asked.

Maybe now she would learn more about this man, his business—or businesses, as the case may be. And his background. She realized she had fallen madly in love with someone she really didn't know anything about. And she had been around long enough to know that things were not always as they seemed.

Although she felt within herself that he was who he seemed, those "feelings" could be proved wrong, if she was blinded by emotion. The other major thing she was judging him on was the fact that he thought she was simply a small-town country girl. He didn't love her for her money or position. He didn't seem to know her business, either.

Yet, she had talked to herself many times about this. He could be playing some elaborate con game. Then she mentally shrugged. She would make no commitments to him until she knew more about him.

She looked at him expectantly, wondering if, and how, he would answer.

Unfortunately, they had reached the door to the dairy building.

"Whew!" he exclaimed. "What an odor! Are they judged on that, too?"

"Of course not!" she said. She realized she wasn't going to get any answers out of him now, but it appeared to have been a major Freudian slip on his part.

Any day now, a report should be coming through from her investigators about who he was. She was patient. She had not achieved all she had in the business world without having that valuable quality.

Brent wasn't sure what he expected as he stepped through the door of the building. He immediately stopped short, looking around.

There was a walkway down the middle of the open building. The walls only came about one-third of the way up on one side. The other side was open, leading off to individual stalls, with water hoses attached to them.

In one stall, a teenager was washing his cow, brushing her down at the same time.

Brent's attention was brought back to the walkway he was on. On either side, cows were haltered, tied to the stalls with their faces toward the walls and their hind ends toward the middle of the building.

One couldn't stand too close and they'd be swatted by a tail swishing at flies or other insects. The cows stood in finely chopped wood chips. There was a large pile of the same type of chips in an empty stall at the beginning of the row.

Light brown cows, dark brown and black cows, spotted cows—some with calves, some without—made up the variety in the barn. Every one of them had bony hips, bony shoulders. He realized he didn't know what a good dairy cow should look like or be judged on. By the look of some of these, they sure did need fattening up.

He said as much to Tali, who laughed at him again and explained that the dairy cows were generally bony. All their energy went to making milk. She admitted she wasn't the perfect judge, either. She just wanted to see who had entered which cows.

She seemed to know so many people here. She stopped at first one set of cows and then another, calling the people by name and admiring their stock. She paid particular attention to the youngsters and teenagers who had their prize pets displayed. She wished each of them good luck. Many of them evidently expected her to be one of the judges but she explained that she wasn't this year. She said she would be judging some of the baking and crafts.

He looked at her questioningly the first time she told someone that. That was the first he had heard about it. But he kept silent. He would wait and see exactly what that was all about. It was bound to be interesting.

He had adjusted to the odor by the time they left that building and entered the next one. It was the beef barn. Here a pleasant surprise awaited him. In contrast to the scrawniness of the milk cows, these steers were beautiful, well-filled-out animals. The ones he admired most were the Santa Gertrudis. They were simply quite imposing animals. Because of their size, they were majestic, stately. He respected that.

From the questions Tali asked, he learned that the price of beef was down at that particular point in time. They had walked through an auction arena between the dairy and beef buildings. Most of these steers would be auctioned off after the judging. There was great pride in who won first, second, and third places. Even better was the one judge to be grand champion. Not only the pride of ownership but also the value of the animal would increase substantially, at least for the bulls, which would most likely be going to stud and not to slaughter.

The grand champion would undoubtedly be auctioned off for stud purposes, Tali explained, breeding further champions. Even if this was just on a county level, that meant future money to these people.

At the most elemental levels, Brent understood the economics and politics he was seeing here. There was no getting away from it, even in the country.

Most of these animals, though, would be sent to slaughter, becoming steaks or hamburgers on dinner tables around the nation. Other by-products would be made from every scrap of them.

It was so hot this summer that most of the cattle had fans blowing on them, some with mist coming from the fans. One person told them that several rabbits had already perished in another building because of the severe heat. The temperature and the rain seemed to be the secondary conversations of most of these people.

Brent was almost ready for the hog barn by the time they reached it.

Almost.

Here in the hog barn, young people were also washing off their pets, trying to keep them clean for the judging. There seemed to be even more varieties of pigs, more colors, than there had been cattle.

Again, as before, many of the people knew Tali. She always had a greeting, some personal word for them. She even knew the names of some of the pigs.

Brent found that amusing. Did she visit these people on a regular basis, or what? Sure, these people around here all knew each other, or of each other, but how could so many know Tali?

After the first "so, how is Becky today?" Brent realized Tali was not talking about a sister or mother. She was talking about the pig on display.

When he commented on her knowing the names of the pigs, Tali just laughed up at him. "Oh, I'm personal friends with most of them."

She was having a good time and her delight was infectious. He realized after a while that he was actually enjoying himself, too. But then, he was always happy when he was with Tali.

They doubled back through the beef barn to get to another area. Brent was in the middle of petting one of the young steers, which his owner said was named "T-bone," when Tali suddenly touched his arm.

"Time to go," she said, looking down at her watch.

"Where to this time?" he asked, giving T-bone one last pat. He had enjoyed talking to the owners and petting the animal.

It wasn't until many heads turned their way and watched them leave the barn that he realized that he, too, had been on display. He overheard a comment of "that's the first time she's ever brought a man anywhere I can recollect."

He knew they were talking about Tali.

Even though he had been in town long enough for some to recognize him, he would now be a great topic of conversation, his name linked with Tali's. He realized that fact didn't bother him at all. In fact, he felt proud to be with her.

"I have to help judge the baked goods and junior craft items. We just have time to get there so I can wash my hands. I let the time get away from me."

She was already several steps ahead of him down the aisle so he hurried to catch up. When they arrived at another building, the group to judge the wares was just forming.

"Tali! Good! We thought for a minute or two you were not going to show. It would not have been the same without you."

Tali smiled her thanks and accepted her pad and pencils. They would be given plates and utensils to try each item when they came to it.

The group started with cooked pie shells. There were only six entries. Tali glanced up at Brent and he mouthed "Six?"

"Takes a lot of skill to make a perfect crust," she said. "Not just anyone can do it well."

She laughed at his look. Didn't every pie shell look the same?

She shook her head at him, turning back to accept a bite from the first one. One by one, the judges walked down the line of each item. They taste tested each one and compared notes. They decided right on the spot, which won the blue ribbon, the red, and the white. It was placed on the item and everything was put back into the glass case. These items would not be eaten by anyone later.

After the judges each had a taste, they were just on display.

Everything went smoothly until they came to the custards. When the winner of the blue ribbon was announced, there was a protest from someone in the crowd that had been following them around.

Since the items were judged, decided on, and then the

nametag turned over, the judges had no way of knowing whose dish they were tasting. This took all favoritism out of the selection.

The blue ribbon for custard went to Tali's Granny and the protest was because the person felt Tali knew which item was her grandmother's. She was accused of choosing that one on purpose. However, Tali appeared just as surprised as anyone when the tag was turned over and her grandmother's name was called out.

"Now, why don't I ever get such wonderful custard at home?" she asked, which brought a laugh from the crowd.

"Now, Marcy, you know better than that," the head judge said, looking at the protestor. "You know Tali wouldn't do that, now, don't you?"

The woman named Marcy had the good grace to look sheepish. "I know, it's just—"

"Disappointing, I know," the head judge finished for her. "We all know. We've all been there, now, haven't we?"

Marcy looked around the crowd, where many heads nodded in agreement.

Tali didn't let the allegation affect her good spirits as the judging went on. In fact, her grandmother won two more blue ribbons. One was for her canned green beans.

Somehow, Brent was not surprised at that one. How could they not win? All Granny seemed to be doing every time he saw her was snap those beans.

She won another ribbon for a knitted sweater in the

crafts section. Since Tali had nothing to do with the judging of the adult crafts, she felt better. She wasn't worried, though. Her grandmother had been winning several ribbons every year at the county fair for as far back as Tali could remember. Something would have seemed more wrong if Granny had not won anything.

After her duty of judging, Tali and Brent viewed the rest of the animals. Time had really flown by. They had come to the fair around dark and now it was really getting late. But the rides would stay open for quite some time.

"Is that all the animals?" he asked, surprised to find that he was almost disappointed.

She looked up at him, smiling. "Disappointed?"

"Yeah, sorta, kinda, I guess I am—maybe a little," he conceded, grinning sheepishly. He really hated to admit he had enjoyed something as simple as a county fair. "But understand, the company had a lot to do with it, you know."

He gave her such a look that her heart leaped. She felt a sudden desire to reach up, put both hands on his face, pull him down to her, and kiss him.

Oh, what the heck, she thought.

That's exactly what she did. Several people walking by smiled at them. A few people called out to them.

"Way to go, Tali. Don't let such a looker get away!"

One young, curvaceous blonde who was undoubtedly showing off the curves she had in a low-cut, off-the-shoulder peasant blouse, stopped beside them.

"Is there enough of that to go around?" she asked, in what she thought was a provocative way. She put her hand on Brent's arm, revealing long, red fingernails.

"No way, Margie," Tali responded. "This one's mine."

"Oh, really?" Margie asked. Her eyes never left Brent's face. Her invitation was unmistakable.

"'Fraid so, ma'am," he replied in his best Southern drawl.

She looked suitably disappointed and turned to Tali. "You always get the good ones. But then, we all know why, don't we?"

She turned and flounced away, stopping a few feet from them, where two young men were tossing a small sized basketball into a smaller-than-regulation net. The idea was to toss a certain number of balls through the net in a certain time. If you beat the clock, you won a price, usually a small, stuffed animal.

"Do we?" he asked Tali, looking down at her.

"Do we what?" she asked innocently, pretending to look over the crowd.

"Know why you always get the 'good ones' as she called it."

"Just lucky, that's all. Or, maybe it's just that I don't try to show all the goods up front, if you'll excuse the pun. Look, I know that sounds bitchy, but Margie's been like that since we were in kindergarten. She's dressed like that longer than I can remember. She doesn't seem to realize that not

all men—especially the 'good ones'—don't always appreciate that sort of dress and come on. Did you?"

He shrugged. "It's par for the course. In a way, I suppose, but mostly you're right. It's always better to have
most of the goods covered, with just enough exposed to tan-
talize the senses, like a tight-fitting T-shirt and cutoffs, perhaps? Then, just put those beautiful legs on a magnificent-
looking horse and *wow*!"

He grinned down at her.

They both remembered that first meeting and smiled at
each other.

"Love at first sight, huh?" she asked. "Just couldn't resist, right?"

"Right," he said, still teasing her. She didn't realize just
how right she was. "Come on, I'll win you the biggest teddy
bear in the whole fair. Even if they only paid five dollars for
it and it takes me two hundred, I'll keep trying 'til I win it
for you."

"Really? You'd do that for little ol' me?" she teased,
putting her hand on his chest. "Moi?"

"You bet!"

Chapter 17

They walked toward the midway, chatting away, their mood light.

Mostly he stared down at her. Although they were in a crowd, they seemed to be all alone. They were so deeply engrossed in each other that they felt as if they were the only two people in the world.

All at once, he happened to look up. He got a shock that almost made him stop in his tracks. The only thing that prevented him from coming to a halt was the fact that Tali would ask why. He could not have explained.

The crowd had parted, as if on cue, and Brent got a brief glimpse of Lily before the throng came together again. That brief glimpse of her seemed to make time stand still.

He was stunned! Yet, why hadn't he thought of this

possibility? Perhaps it was because Lily had asked him if he would like to come home with her *this weekend*—home, meaning to Granville—and come to the county fair with her. He had turned her down, sounding appropriately regrettable with a plausible excuse, hoping to be with Tali most of this weekend.

Had he allowed himself to even think about it, he would have thought Lily safely at work in the city in the middle of the week. He had to admit he hadn't given Lily a second thought as soon as he was on his way to Tali.

Lily's head had been turned. She had been laughing up at the man she was with and hadn't seen Brent, but they had been coming this way. The crowd could part at any second, giving her a full view of him and Tali. That certainly wouldn't do! He didn't want a confrontation with her at this point. He had only a second to decide what to do.

He and Tali were in front of a space, a narrow alleyway between the two canvas tents of two sideshows, so he put his arm around her waist and led her quickly between them.

"Wha—" Tali began, but he stopped her a few steps into the area, kissing her long and thoroughly.

She melted against him, just as she always did when he kissed her like this. She just couldn't seem to resist him.

He made a point of making sure her back was to the opening onto the midway. He let her go, but still held her, looking deeply into her eyes, keeping her attention completely on him. He seemed to be getting very good at deception!

"Well, I didn't know a county fair could be so inspiring," she said, smiling up at him.

"You're the one who's inspiring, wherever you are," he returned. "What do you say we get out of here? We've been here long enough, don't you think?"

He reached for her again.

She had been here long enough a while back, but had not said anything to him, wanting him to thoroughly enjoy his first experience at a fair such as this.

But she pushed him away, gently. "Oh, no," she responded. "Not here. Not again."

"Not here?" he questioned. "Why not?"

"Well, the people around here just don't go in for a lot of public displays of affection. We both know if you kissed me again, it would not be a simple kiss. You know what your touch does to me."

"I do?" he asked, looking into her eyes.

His desire and passion suddenly flared. She saw this in his eyes and took a small step backward. "Oh, no, you don't," she repeated, but she was smiling.

"Let's stay out of the crowd," he said.

"Oh, no," she said, pulling him back as he started to turn them away from the crowd.

"I want a teddy bear. Didn't you promise?"

"I'll give you something much better," he whispered, taking a step toward her.

She took another step backward. "Later," she said,

huskily. "Later, okay? I don't want you to miss this experience of coming to a county fair. We haven't played any of the games or gone on any of the rides yet. Don't you want to do that?"

He sighed, backing off. "So, what do I do about this?"

She knew what he was talking about and blushed. It would take several minutes before he could go out into the crowd.

"Deal with it," she said, pretending indifference.

"Can you just turn your emotions on and off like that?" he asked, snapping his fingers.

"No," she replied, her voice almost a whisper. "But I try to control them. There's a time and place for everything. This is *not* the time. I have to live with these people. Let's not do anything to make that hard for me, okay?"

"You're right, of course," he agreed. "Let's walk up to the beginning of the midway this back way. That'll give me time."

It would also give Lily and her friend time to be at this end. He just hoped and prayed that they did not turn around and immediately head back the way they had come. There was another part of the midway, across from this one, with several kiosks and free-standing food "shacks" making up a middle row. There was no set way the crowd moved. They just milled back and forth as they wished. There was no such thing as staying to the right.

Perhaps because of this random moving around the

four of them would never run into each other.

Starting with the first booth they came to, they played several different types of games before Brent was able to win anything for Tali. Then it was only a small stuffed animal.

They laughed at this.

They chose several different rides. Then they decided it was time to go.

So, they made their way slowly behind the tents and through the main gate to the car.

He had held his breath all the way, hoping Lily would not spot them. He thanked the gods when they made it safely to the pickup and had turned onto the main highway. Granny had gotten a ride with a friend, and so they were alone.

On the way home, he turned into a dirt road he had noticed several times. It was a road going off to the right before they came into view of the farmhouse.

She looked over at him questioningly.

He put his fingers to his lips, asking her to be silent.

He drove far enough down so that the main road was no longer in sight. A dogleg turn to the right had helped that. He brought the pickup to a halt. "Where does this road go?" he asked her.

He turned to her, putting his arm across the back of the seat. He touched the back of her neck with his hand, gently caressing her neck and stroking her hair.

"Nowhere," she said, shrugging. "Just a road hunters use sometime. Long ago there was a house on up a little bit because there is an old chimney still standing. In the spring, what used to be a front yard is alive with jonquils. But there's nothing there now. TD and I have explored it many times. We don't get too close to the old home site, though, just in case there's an old well, or something like that, hidden in the undergrowth."

"Good," he said, leaning toward her. "I always wanted to kiss a beautiful lady in a pickup deep in the woods with no one else around."

"Oh, really," she said, leaning toward him in response. "Are you sure you don't want to get in the back seat?"

"Well…" he answered, playing the game. He looked over the seat to the king cab area behind them. "Actually, I'm not sure we would fit. You maybe, but not me."

They both laughed. His six-foot-two frame certainly would not fit in that space.

"I have a blanket in the back," she said, whispering. Inviting.

"Really?" he asked. "Do you always come prepared for such times?"

"It always stays in here. It comes in handy for a lot of things," was her response.

Without saying another word, he reached over the seat and retrieved the blanket. He got out and went around to help her down.

As she emerged from the cab, before she was standing upright on the ground, he had his arms around her. As she looked up at him, his lips found hers and they embraced passionately. Their kiss seemed to go on forever.

She felt his passion rise, not only by his kiss, but also by the hardness against her. She reached down and touched him, gently caressing him.

He moaned, breaking the kiss and leading her to a clear spot under some trees. He spread the blanket for them. They went down on their knees, touching each other in a gentle caress. He started to unbutton her blouse as they kissed again. She reached out to undo his belt, then his zipper. They could not stop here, even if they wanted to, which neither of them did.

Their passion rose to such a crescendo that they lost all thought of where they were. It didn't matter. All they knew was the touch, the feel, and smell of each other.

The softness of Tali's skin excited Brent almost beyond control.

At the height of their lovemaking, when they could hold out no longer, both cried out in unison, clinging to each other. Brent felt Tali's nails dig into the skin of his back but the sensation brought pleasure, not pain. He knew she did so out of passion.

Their energy spent, they lay entwined in each other's arms, breathing heavily. Brent's hand rested just below Tali's left breast. He felt her heart pounding. He left his hand there as his own heart slowed to its normal rhythm.

Neither was inclined to move. They both enjoyed the post-love time they had together. It was as much a part of their love as any part of their lovemaking. They felt even closer than ever at this special time.

Finally, Brent rose up on one elbow, his head resting on his hand. He looked down at her, his eyes filled with love.

He kissed her again, lingeringly.

She sat up, gently pushing him away. "Granny's been home for a while now. Let's go see if we can find your tape."

"Oh, yeah, the tape," he agreed. He had forgotten all about the tape during the time at the fair and now this time with her. He had forgotten everything but being with her. "You're right. Time to go."

When they arrived at the house, Granny had bad news for them. The boy who had borrowed the tape had accident-ly taped over it.

Brent couldn't believe it. How could someone have such little regard for the property of others? He said as much.

"He really felt bad, he did," Granny said. "Just couldn't say he was sorry enough. I couldn't scold him because he felt so awful about doing it. He's even offered to buy you another copy of *Beetlejuice,* since that's what he thought it was. Can you get another tape like the one you had?"

"No, I'm afraid not," he said. "It was a one-of-a-kind."

"You say it was of Mrs. Barnett? At her offices?" Tali asked.

"Yes, it was. We were finally going to see what she looked like."

"And how were you able to get that? I've heard she has pretty upscale security in her buildings."

Tali tried to sound very casual, not too interested. She really wanted to know the answer, of course, so she could make sure it wouldn't happen again.

"Trade secret," he said, grinning, and changed his voice to a Russian accent. "Ve have our Vays."

"We? Who's we?" she asked.

"Just us boys," he said, laughing. He had to laugh, otherwise he would be so angry at the boy he would have to leave.

Seeing Lily at the fair had given him another idea of how to get photos of Mrs. Barnett. Evidently being with Lily in Granville, with the possibility of being seen with her, was too risky. He had enjoyed the dinner with her, though, when he was in the city. That he would continue, hoping to learn more about Mrs. Barnett.

He left with his idea gaining credence as he drove along.

He had not seen the look that had passed between Tali and Granny. For a while, at least, Tali's secret was safe once more.

Chapter 18

Brent made several more trips to the old plantation. He hoped to catch a glimpse of the occupants, assuming one of them would be Mrs. Barnett. This seemed a likely place for her home. He needed to be here long enough to get some photos. He had rented a high-tech camera with a telescopic lens.

He hadn't asked to use the old Ford pickup of Burt's again. Each time he came down now he had rented a different four-wheel drive in the city and had come in this back way. He didn't want to be seen in the same vehicle and arouse suspicions. This way the locals would just think someone was hunting.

After a week of coming off and on, however, he had been unable to get any photos. Once a light had gone on in one of the upper rooms when he was out in the evening. He watched a silhouette go back and forth for a while but was not able to pinpoint anything.

He had even climbed the fence and been close to the house several times. He came close to being caught once when a window suddenly opened and someone poured some water out and down on the flower bed where he was standing.

He finally gave up. He decided that there were surely better ways of getting what he needed.

He hoped.

Chapter 19

The man walked out the side door of the building and stopped a few feet away. He patted the pockets of his coveralls, obviously looking for his cigarettes.

Brent saw the man's mouth move as he got out of the car. He could imagine what the man was saying.

Brent did not smoke but he had brought some cigarettes with him for just this purpose. For several days, he had watched various men on the maintenance crew take their breaks and this man was the one he wanted.

Brent approached him. "Cigarette?" he asked, holding out his pack.

"Yeah, man, you're a life saver. Must have left mine somewhere."

Sure, you did. Brent had learned that this was the man's daily routine and that enabled him to mooch off the other men. He also used the lighter Brent offered to him.

"I'm Brent," he offered by way of conversation. "You work here?"

"Yep," was the reply. "Tony."

"Some building," Brent said, looking up. It was almost a matter of looking straight up.

"Sure is," Tony agreed. He was already wondering what Brent wanted. As Brent looked up at the building, Tony looked at Brent. A guy dressed like this always wanted something.

"Guess you pretty much know your way around the place," Brent offered.

Tony shrugged, giving the interpretation of consent. But he wasn't admitting to anything yet.

"Thought you might be willing to help me out with something," Brent began, looking across the street.

Both men knew they had to appear in casual conversation, nothing serious. To anyone watching, it would be an executive and a maintenance worker having a smoke together. These smoke breaks made strange bed partners, so to speak.

"Oh, yeah? Like what?"

"The owner of this building."

"Say, who?" Tony asked, pretending not to know who Brent meant.

"You know what she looks like?"

"Could be, maybe not."

"Can you get near her for a while, long enough to take some pictures, without being noticed? I happen to know maintenance men are usually ignored."

"Ain't it the truth?" the man agreed.

Both men were silent for a few seconds.

"Yeah, I know where she is most of the time."

"Thought so," Brent said.

Tony nodded. So, Brent had done his homework. He did want something. Tony was becoming more and more interested in what that might be.

Brent could see Tony was taking the bait.

"That's all you want, just some pictures of the old lady?" Tony asked.

"That's it," Brent agreed. "I want quite a few, though, from different angles. Can you get real close?"

Tony shrugged. "Yeah, pretty close. Like you said, maintenance men are invisible. Camera's pretty obvious, though. This ain't someone you can just walk up to, say 'cheese' and snap a picture."

"I know. That's why I have this."

Brent held up a lunch pail, the kind with a place for a thermos bottle built into the lid. It looked like a typical working man's lunch bucket.

Tony had wondered about it. Brent had been holding it while they talked. It just didn't go with the silk suit the man was wearing. Brent wouldn't carry his lunch to work in a pail.

If he worked at all.

Tony doubted that he did.

"This is not a thermos," Brent began. "This is really a video camera. The whole lunch pail is a video camera. It can take two hours of video. A lunch pail can go in lots of places a camera can't. No metal, so it passes the security gate without setting off an alarm. Just your typical lunch pail, that's all."

Typical, my ass, Tony thought. *If this man has the money to come up with this cute little toy, then something is going down.* "Sorry, man, I can't get into anything illegal. I'm on parole. Can't get caught doing a thing."

"Nothing illegal," Brent assured him. "Just taking a video of the party we mentioned, that's all. The most anyone could do if they realized what you were doing would be to take the video tape out, and you wouldn't get the photos. Everybody wants pictures of the rich and famous. But you won't get caught," Brent continued, assuring him. "You're too smart for that. That's why I picked you for the job."

Tony knew Brent was blowing sunshine up his rear but it still had the desired effect on him. Brent was right. Tony knew he was too smart to get caught. This man wanted this video so badly, Tony knew he was willing to pay for it. How much would be the next question. "Must be really important to you," he said, taking a pull on his cigarette. Good cigarette. The man didn't buy generic ones, that was for sure.

Now it began.

They both knew how to play the game. Now it was just a matter of how much Tony wanted and how much Brent was willing to pay.

"You might say that," Brent answered. "How does $10,000 sound to you?"

Ten big ones? The man was willing to pay that much for a few minutes of film?

"You need the full two hours?" he ventured.

"I need some good, clean shots of the face, head and shoulders. Smiling, unsmiling. If it takes the full two hours, then so be it. If you think you've got it in a few minutes, then fine. You might have to take shots at different times. I'll leave that up to you."

Ten thousand for two hours of work wasn't bad. But accepting the first offer wasn't a part of the game. Tony knew Brent had started at the low end. He could get more.

They settled for $12,000.

Brent handed Tony the lunch pail. Tony would get the money when the job was done. Brent would be back here at the same place, sometime next week. That would give Tony plenty of time to get some good shots.

"And, Tony," Brent concluded, as he handed him the camera. "Don't con me. You are on parole, right?"

Tony knew what Brent was saying. "You'll get the video, man, don't worry," he assured him. He dropped his cigarette on the concrete. He crushed it with his foot and turned to walk back into the building. *Frickin' rich people.* Yeah, he'd get the photos of the old lady for the guy. It was good money. But he hated the threat. It was people like that who had put him in prison the first time. Thought they were better than anyone else.

Brent didn't realize he had made an enemy when he made the threat.

For the next week taking videos of Mrs. Barnett was a piece of cake for Tony. He even enjoyed doing it without being detected. Before he met Brent to give him his tape, he made himself a copy of it. If this rich turkey was so willing to pay so much for it, there was probably more in it for Tony, too. It was just a matter of figuring out what.

What a gold mine! Tony thought, as he copied the video.

Not only was Brent's name on the film but Tony caught on immediately to what was happening. Mrs. Barnett was not *Mrs*. Barnett. Nor was she an elderly woman.

Tony had a friend who wrote for one of those gossip rags that would really pay for this. Well, he wouldn't, of course, but the magazine would. But Tony was smart enough to wait to see what Brent was going to do with the tape.

Twelve thousand was peanuts.

Tony was going to be rich!

Chapter 20

The small viewing room was dark. The only light came from a small light over the computer keyboard.

Brent had brought the video tape to a friend who could plug it into his company's computer and project the image on a large-screen TV built into the wall. This way, Brent would have an excellent view of what the tape contained.

He just hoped the images on the tape were going to be worth the $12,000 he had paid for it. Tony had taken the whole two hours, or at least he said he had. Brent just hoped he got one decent shot.

Suddenly the film was on. It revealed someone coming out of the same office door that he had staked out.

This time the woman had on a large floppy hat, which

covered half her face. That wasn't Tony's fault, of course. There was no way he could know what Mrs. Barnett would be wearing at any given time.

About that time, evidently someone came down the hall from the opposite way and called to her, because she turned away from the camera. For the next several minutes, she talked to someone with her back turned to them.

The film went dead. At least Tony had enough sense to know that if she was going to stand and talk with her back to him for the next hour, he should turn off the camera.

Once again the film started, this time showing her getting into a car on the outside of the building. But for several more minutes the film was not close enough, or clear enough, to get a good shot of her face.

Off again.

"Is there anything worth watching on this tape?" his friend asked. He turned it off momentarily as he turned toward Brent.

"I sure hope so. I paid enough for it," Brent replied.

"What are looking for? Something special?"

"I would really like to get a good, clear shot of her face to see what she really looks like. No one has been able to get a good photo of her at all, much less her face. I want to be the first. Also, she told me personally she had a man in her life, so if the guy got one good shot of them together, it would be worth it."

"This is really important to you, huh?" the friend asked.

"Yeah—" Brent started but the film came back on.

There it was. A full face shot of her as she came out of her office door again and started down the hall toward the man.

It couldn't be. This couldn't be Mrs. Barnett.

"Stop it. Can you stop it?" he asked his friend excitedly.

The friend froze the frame immediately at his request.

"Now, how can that be?" Brent asked out loud, but he was really talking to himself.

"What?" the friend asked. "You wanted a good, head-on shot of her face. I'd say you're looking at it. It doesn't get much better than that." The frame showed a beautiful face framed by the same floppy hat as before. "But I thought you said this woman was an older woman. This certainly isn't an elderly woman."

"No, it sure isn't," Brent agreed.

He leaned back in his chair, his head cocked to one side, staring at Tali on the screen. It was definitely Tali. There was no denying that. He would have recognized her anywhere. And if her face was not enough, there were little wisps of hair, coming out from under a wig that had obviously been put on in haste. Auburn hair.

She was laughing at someone behind her who had come out of the office with her.

He sat, stunned. True, Tali had admitted that she knew Mrs. Barnett. Perhaps she was just visiting the old woman and the man let the video run before he realized he had the wrong person.

Of course. That was it.

"Start it up again, Tom. Let's see some more. This can't be her."

His friend started the tape and they watched as Tony moved aside as she went by, still with the camera rolling.

"Hello, how are you today?" Tali's voice.

He also took pictures of her as she walked away, moving the camera up and down. Shapely legs were revealed on the tape.

Tali's legs, for sure. Hadn't he caressed those beautiful, shapely legs?

The camera stopped again then started up as the elevator door opened and "Mrs. Barnett" once again walked toward him toward her office door.

Another full-face shot.

"Stop it here," he said to his friend.

There was no mistaking it. It was Tali.

But was it Mrs. Barnett?

"Okay," he said and his friend started the video again.

The man again took up and down angles, including one of something she was holding up to her chest. It was a book or something.

But it was not the book or whatever the woman had in her hand that Brent was interested in. "Wait!" Brent cried. "Right there."

Tom stopped it on a view of her hand.

Her right hand.

There it was. If he thought before perhaps he was just seeing a look-alike of Tali, then this was his proof that it was, indeed, Tali.

There on the pinkie finger of her right hand was her great-grandmother's ring.

"Whew! What a ring," Tom said, as he gave a low whistle. "Custom made, for sure. Worth a fortune. Look at those diamonds. And what else is that?"

"Rubies," Brent said.

"Yeah, could be," the friend agreed.

"It is, believe me. I know," Brent said.

"You know? If you know, why did you need this tape? I thought you didn't know what she looked like."

"I didn't. Or at least I didn't know what Mrs. Barnett looked like."

"Huh?" asked his friend. "Say again."

"Either this man with the camera really conned me or this really is Mrs. Barnett."

"Want to see the rest of it?"

"Sure," Brent agreed.

He sat through the rest of the tape. He had his friend stop the tape at a few spots and then run a still print. He was already formulating an idea.

Tali had told him that day of the interview, after the wonderful time at the creek, that there was a new man in her life. She had said it as Mrs. Barnett. Was the old man in the video the love of her life? And if it were, where did that leave him? Hadn't Tali told Brent she loved him?

Hadn't Tali said to him, as Tali, that she was "head-over-heels" in love with him? Yet that was the same expression, she had used as Mrs. Barnett.

He really wasn't sure what to think about that at this point.

Did Tali love him as Tali? Did Tali love someone else as Mrs. Barnett? Were there two men in her life?

He needed more information. Something just wasn't right here.

The next day, he was waiting outside the same building where he had talked to Tony before. He wasn't sure if Tony would be there. A guy like that might take the money and become smoke.

Tony stepped out the door and stopped when he saw Brent.

"Tape okay?" he asked casually.

"Got a serious question for you," Brent said.

Tony acted as if he didn't hear him. He was hunting for his usual non-existent cigarette.

"Here." Brent practically shoved the cigarette into the man's hand. "I asked you to video a certain person—" he began.

"Don't tell me the film was bad. You gave it to me," Tony retorted.

"The film was fine. It was who you filmed that was the problem."

"Hey, you said you wanted Mrs. B. You got Mrs. B. Front, back, side, every angle I could get to. Quite a looker, huh?"

"That's just it. That's not Mrs. B., as you call her. That's a beautiful young lady on the tape."

"Yeah? So?" the man asked. "What's your problem?"

"Mrs. B. is an older woman."

The man threw back his head and laughed. "That's what a lot of people think," he said. "You're wrong, you know. Mrs. B. is not even 'Mrs.' B. Make that 'Ms.' B. and you have it. You're wrong about another thing, too."

Brent just looked at him questioningly.

"You said before that maintenance men are invisible, no one notices them. In a way that's true, but not with Mrs. B. She always stops and says hello, asks me how I'm doing. She notices things. A camera in a lunch box was just ingenious, that's all." He paused. "You know, I almost didn't take the pictures of her for you, but—"

"Okay, okay," Brent said impatiently. "So, what color hair does Mrs. B. have?"

Tony shrugged, thinking. "Auburn? Is that what you call it? Not a redhead, really. Just a pretty dark red, sort of."

Tali.

"And beautiful legs. Don't forget those beautiful legs."

How could he forget them?

"Need some more?" Tony asked.

"No, I'm okay. Just wasn't sure who I was seeing on the tape, that's all. Thanks, man."

Brent walked away, leaving Tony staring after him. Tony wasn't sure what to think about this whole situation yet. He would wait and see. He had all the time in the world.

He wasn't going anywhere.

Chapter 21

Brent sat that evening in his apartment. He was starting to put all the things together, from the first meeting with Tali up to the tape.

What was Tali's last name? He frowned. He realized he didn't even know her last name. He had told her his complete name but she had simply said "Tali." Granny had been introduced only as "Granny Mae."

All those times that Tali wasn't in Granville. Then the helicopter showed up and after that, he saw Tali. Everybody knew Tali. And that's why they protected her. She was their hometown girl who became rich and famous. The family probably had old money and land to begin with and, with smart business deals, had amassed a fortune.

By never forgetting her "roots," Tali endeared herself

in the hearts of those people. So, they kept her secret.

The more he thought about it, the more he was convinced that she had made a fool of him. He didn't know she was Mrs. Barnett and she had decided to play with him with that knowledge.

What a stupid fool he had been! By putting all the facts as he knew them together with the clues he now had, it all made perfect sense. No wonder Lily said she had grown up with her. They were the same age. Probably had been in kindergarten together.

They probably had a big laugh about him every time Tali came to the city. What a laugh she must have had over his puny endeavors to get an interview from Mrs. Barnett. And who had given him that interview? He remembered the beginning of it, how the voice sounded so familiar before it changes, and then there were the same expression they both used.

All the clues had been there if he had just been smart enough to see then, to put them together.

But then, his brain had been in the wrong spot.

And Tandy Dan. Of course, that made sense now, also. Tandy Dan belonged to Tali, she didn't just train him. Thinking back, though, every answer Tali gave was the truth. It just wasn't *all* the truth.

He decided to write the article and submit it for publication along with the photos. He decided to win The Game. But he wasn't sure what to do about Tali. He knew he still loved her but he had loved her as Tali, the country girl. He wasn't sure how he felt about Tali the big city business woman and owner of a fortune.

Hell, her wealth was much more than his and that was really saying something. And he had been ready to ask Tali to marry him and take her out of the country. He knew that would never happen now.

Why didn't she tell him? That's what he couldn't figure out. Obviously, she knew he had money.

Why didn't she tell him? She knew he didn't know who she was. That question just kept going around and around in his head. He couldn't stop it. But he had no answers.

He knew he would write the article.

She would never make a fool of him again. The more he thought about it, the angrier he became.

He would show her.

Chapter 22

Brent spent the next several days in his apartment. He wrote and rewrote the article about Tali, or Mrs. Barnett, or both. He typed page after page, then he crumbled it up, and threw it in the wastebasket. Not all his shots hit the target. There was a growing pile of wadded up paper around the wastebasket.

He ignored them. He had not eaten anything these past two days. All his time and energy had been spent on just how to write the article.

He wondered if Tali missed him. He had not called and he certainly had not gone to Granville for five days now. He missed her so much he had almost walked out the door many times on his way there.

But he had resisted.

Chapter 23

Tali was curled up on the sofa in her penthouse when there was a rapid, impatient tapping on the door.

"Tali? Tali? Open up!"

It was Lily.

This was early morning. Tali glanced at the clock. Seven a.m.

She moved rapidly to the door. Something had to be wrong to bring Lily to her door this early, even if she were in the next apartment.

Lily was through the door before Tali had it completely open.

"You won't believe this! You really won't. You haven't seen it or I would be hearing about it, I know."

"What?"

Lily was so excited. She hadn't even been this uptight talking about this new boyfriend of hers. She held up a tabloid, waving it in the air. "Look," she said, moving over to the coffee table and slamming the paper down. She pointed. "There!"

On the front of the tabloid was the headline:

Mystery Woman Unveiled!

The subtitle was:

The Elusive Margaret Barnett is cornered!

There on the front page was a terrible photo of Tali coming out of her office doors, complete with wig and scarf. But the face was definitely hers.

Tali was in shock for a few seconds. How could this be? How did it happen?

"You're kidding!" She finally found her voice. But now she couldn't think of even one word.

Exclusive photos inside the subtitle continued. *See why Margaret Barnett isn't who she says she is!*

"Who did this?" she was able to ask. "Who? I want his, or her, head. Immediately. It has to be someone in the building. Someone close enough to be able to take photos."

A mental picture of a handsome young janitor working

the hall with toolboxes and a lunch box on the floor around him came to Lily's mind. But she dismissed it as Tali was continuing, giving out orders of what to do about this.

"I certainly hope this rag has good malpractice insurance, 'cause they're going to need it!"

By the end of the day, Tali had the information she wanted.

Brent!

The informant on the magazine let her know that a man who said his name was Brent Walker let him have a copy of a video and other info about her hometown.

Brent!

Her anger died down a little by early evening. She wasn't sure if her anger was worse than the hurt this produced, though. They seemed to be running neck to neck right now.

He must never have loved her as he had said. He had only used her, her feelings, to get the information he wanted. Lily had made the connection, of course. She remembered Tali's reaction whenever this Brent called the office, which he had done a few times over the past two months. She knew Tali's hurt was greater than any anger she had.

Businesswise, Tali could ruin this "yellow dog journalism" rag if she really wanted to. But what did you do with a broken heart?

By evening, they were back in Tali's apartment. Had this only been one day? It seemed like forever.

"Where is he now?" Lily asked.

Tali was standing in front of her balcony window, staring out. Her stare and mind were blank.

"Tali?"

She turned around, still in a daze.

"Where is he now? Brent? Where is he?"

"Oh, I don't know," Tali finally responded. "He said he did have to make a living and would be gone for a few days. If he's wise, he'll stay gone, of course."

But hadn't she done the same thing? Didn't she go away on her own business whenever she wanted to or needed to? They had not told each other when they were leaving or returning. They had been too independent for that. Looking back, it was a wonder they had both showed up at the same time in the same place at all.

Then she started having suspicions. How did he always manage to be in Granville when she was?

Of course! He probably had her spied on all along. The ultimate reward of all the spying was his photographs. He had undoubtedly sold them to the highest bidder.

At least he had been correct about one thing. He was *not* a journalist, not even a small-time reporter. No one calling himself a journalist would sell to the mag rags!

No, she didn't know where he was right now. And she told herself she didn't care.

"Did he do this often? Just go away for a few days at a time, I mean? And not saying where he was going?"

"Yeah, several times since I've known him. How was I to know he was coming to this building at the same time I was, lurking in the halls to get photos of 'Mrs. Barnett'?"

Again, the image of Michael flashed through Lily's mind. She frowned. *I wonder…*

She didn't have time to continue her thought as Tali abruptly sat down on her sofa, leaned forward with her face in her hands, and started crying in deep, loud sobs.

Lily stood there, feeling helpless. She had never seen her friend cry like this. Not even when Tali lost her dog when she was twelve. The dog had been with her since birth.

Lily herself could not hold back the tears. She cried with her friend. Although Tali had never said much about Brent, Lily knew her feelings. When Tali had finally fallen for a man, it had been hard and completely.

It wasn't like Tali to be such a bad judge of character. But who could judge love? Love was blind and could make a person do funny things—things they might never do normally.

They simply had to cry it out.

Chapter 24

Brent was the first to arrive. He was shown to a table in a raised alcove at the back of the restaurant. He was in the middle of his first drink when the first of four other men showed up.

"Brent! How's it going, man? Any luck?"

"Dave," Brent said, acknowledging the man as he took a seat at the opposite side of the table. "Sorry, you'll just have to wait 'til the others get here to hear about any progress I made. You?"

Dave laughed. "Patience, patience. If I have to wait, then so do you."

In a few minutes, two other men came in together, greeting Brent and Dave heartily.

Only one remained.

They decided to order drinks and appetizers. The fifth man would just have to be late.

These four men were the reason Brent had ended up with a flat on a dirt road in what he first thought was the middle of nowhere. They had been friends with Brent since college. They had all been in the same frat house. The one not yet there was the one who had originally thought up the idea of The Game that they now all played.

They met socially off and on, through their businesses, and often just as friends. They met together once a year for this specific purpose, though.

The idea one had come up with was that each of them would think up a "project." This project could not be a piece of cake. It had to be worthy of the talent, time, and money each would expend on it. It would not necessarily have to be hard enough to take them away from their respective businesses. They understood the importance of making money. Unfortunately, only two of them had enough family money, independent wealth that they did not have to work at something.

Brent was one of those two.

The project had to be so involved that it took a whole year to complete.

There was always a deadline.

This meeting was the appointed time for each one to report on the success or failure of his endeavor. To begin, each presented the "game plan," in report form, in a plain, unmarked report folder. They were then numbered and each man drew a number. They were not allowed to draw their own report. As each looked at the number, he would say if it was his or not. If it was, he would then draw another. They referred to these as the "challenges."

Brent's challenge for the past year had been to seek out and get a personal interview *and* photographs of the elusive Margaret Barnett, head of PrintCore and heir to a newspaper fortune. She was already fabulously wealthy in her own right and would be even more when her father passed away. She had been made chairman of the board of her family's privately-held corporation.

Brent had to not only get an interview, but get an article published in some national magazine, along with photos. The rule didn't say the magazine had to be reputable or not.

Each assignment could contain only one clue to get the man started. His clue had been: Granville.

It had taken him a whole month just to find the right Granville. He had a lot to say when he found out who had submitted this assignment. Had the man known there were fourteen states with a Granville? Probably not, but it had made it harder.

There was a prize for the winner of this game, of course. The man, or men, who successfully completed their challenges, based on the judgment of the group, was given cash. Each man had to give $10,000 to "play." The money was divided among those who completed the game. One year four had been successful. Another year, only two had finished their challenges.

Brent didn't mind losing this year. He was not going to reveal to the world or even to his four friends who Mrs. Barnet really was.

They only way to convince Tali that he really loved her for herself was to never let her know he knew she was the real "Mrs. Barnett." Maybe someday, when they both were so secure in their love that nothing could harm them, maybe then he would tell her he had found out.

But not now.

The men were laughing, having a good time. Two of the men had won and were asking the others to "divvy up." These two had explained how they had done it. Most of it was pretty funny stuff.

"Hey, aren't we forgetting someone?" one of the asked.

"What do you mean?"

"Brent," the man replied.

Brent looked startled, glancing quickly up at the man. Did he know? How could he?

"I know you're loaded, old boy, but it seems a shame not to get your share of the bet."

"But I didn't—"

He didn't have a chance to finish his denial. His friend reached down and then flopped one of the national tabloids onto the center of the table. "Read it and weep, gentlemen," he said.

"Hey, look at this!" one said. He had entered this assignment, so he recognized it immediately. "You did it, Brent. And you weren't even going to tell us all about it?"

His voice had a false hurt note in it.

"Hey, man, congratulations! Let's see that."

They all leaned forward to see the photos while one of the men read the headlines then the article out loud, turning to the continuing pages.

Brent sat stunned.

True. There it was in black and white. The article even had his name on the by-line, as the author. As the man read, Brent recognized the article he had written. At one time, he had fully intended to submit the article to some magazine, somewhere. This one would not have been his choice, however. But he had changed his mind. His love for Tali had outweighed any game. And the $10,000 prize meant nothing to him, either.

His house had been broken into and several items of jewelry stolen. But he had not even thought to look in the middle drawer of his roll-top desk when he itemized the stolen items for the police. After all, that drawer only contained a stapler, scotch tape, various pens and pencils, that sort of thing. No thief took junk like that. He assumed the envelope with the article and photos was still in the back of the drawer, so the drawer had remained unopened during the investigation. Who knew that article was there?

No one knew that he could think of. No one, of course,

except the one man in this circle who had submitted the idea.

What a stupid, suspicious mind he had. How could he even suspect his friends? Even the one who submitted it didn't know who drew it. They did not tell their challenges until right now, this evening of the deadline, when they proved their success or admitted defeat.

Yet, there it was, in black and white. At least the print was in black and white. The copies of the photos, of course, were in color.

Full, living color.

He was still speechless.

There was no way Tali could avoid seeing this. And there was his name. Someone had even used his name. Yes, you could call yourself whatever you wanted to, use any pseudonym you wanted. But who was dumb enough to use the name of the true author? Yet, on the other hand, why not?

"Well, there goes my $25,000," said one of the men. "Hey, divide that $50,000 again!"

One man took the checks of all five and then wrote the three winners their checks.

Chapter 25

Brent wrote his check and accepted the other with no memory of having done so. The others were so jovial and had enough drinks in them that they did not notice he was unusually quiet. He managed to smile and get through the evening. They were to meet in another month with new game plans for the following year.

How had he made it through the rest of the evening after seeing the article? He had to get to a phone, had to call Tali. The magazine had hit the stands that morning. There was no way she hadn't been told or seen it. Maybe she even bought that rag herself.

He couldn't imagine her doing so, however. It just wasn't her style.

Would she believe that he had decided not to publish

the article? Would she believe that he was willing to lose $10,000 and say he lost?

There was no way she would believe that someone broke into his home and stole a manuscript, for God's sake.

Hell, he wouldn't even believe it himself if he were on the other side. He had spent months trying to get an interview with Mrs. Barnett. No one in his right mind would not sell the article after spending all that time and effort to get it.

So, okay, he wasn't in his right mind. Not as far as Tali was concerned, that was for sure. But now she would never believe that he loved her for her, not because she was Mrs. Matilda Barnett.

There was no way to prove how long he had known she was Mrs. Barnett. After all, it took a while to write an article. She would never believe he wrote and rewrote it for several days after he found out who she was. She would never believe he decided not to use it, had pushed it to the back of a drawer.

And he had finally convinced her how much he loved her. He was sure of that. And he still loved her as Tali, not as Mrs. Barnett. Could he even love her as Mrs. Barnett?

He knew her well enough now to know what her reaction to this article would be.

After dinner, as the others left the restaurant, Brent stopped to use the phone. He left a message for her to call him, leaving his apartment number. He spent all the next day trying to call her but did not get a response. His only hope was to go to Granville, knowing she would probably go there.

But she was not in Granville. He believed Granny when she said she didn't know where Tali was.

He spent the next week trying to call her, to no avail. He was desperate to see her, to talk to her. He finally decided if a maintenance man got the photos the first time, maybe it would work again, to enable him to physically get to her office.

Chapter 26

Tali and Lily came into the office through the hall door, chatting away as they did so.

The temporary secretary they had hired to answer the phones while they were gone rose to her feet and tried to get their attention, but they were too engrossed in their conversation to be distracted. They walked into Tali's inner office.

The temp was trying to tell them there was a maintenance man in Tali's office. He had been dressed correctly and had a work order. She had only been there two days and had let him in.

Tali and Lily did not see the man at first. He was even with the door against the wall.

They had walked to the other end of the room, and Tali

had gone around behind her desk before she turned around and saw him.

"You—" she began, then stopped, speechless and unable to continue.

She had refused to acknowledge his messages or answer his calls. She had not returned to Granville in all this time.

He had completely broken her heart. She told herself she never wanted to see him again. Yet, she had gone over and over in her mind what she would say to him if she did ever see him.

Now she could think of nothing.

Lily had whirled around at the look on her friend's face and her exclamation. She gasped. "You!" she also said.

"You know him?" Tali asked. She frowned. Had they ever been together when he could have met Lily? No, she was sure they had never run into her.

"Know him? I'm dating him!"

"What?" Tali said. She sat down, stunned, gripping the messages she had picked up, crushing them into a ball. "What do you mean?"

At the same time, Brent stepped forward into the center of the room.

"Tali—" he began.

"Tali?" Lily asked. "You know her as Tali?"

He just nodded, giving Lily a look that said he was sorry. "Yes."

"And you know him as…" Tali left the question open-ended.

"Michael, of course," Lily finished for her. She turned to Brent. "You bastard," she began. "You used me. You only used me. You were trying to get to Tali, or Mrs. Barnett, through me, weren't you? Weren't you? Admit it!" She had taken several short steps toward him then stopped. "Oh!" she cried. She threw herself on the sofa in the room, bent over, crying with great sobs. They could barely make out "And I thought you loved me," through her crying.

Brent and Tali just looked at each other. The seconds seemed like hours to Brent.

Tali's mind was racing. She pictured him making love to Lily like he had to her and she was numb with the thought.

"It was a game," he said.

"A game! A game!" Tali exclaimed, rising from her chair. She slapped her palms on her desk. "A game," she repeated. She wanted to pick up everything on her desk and throw them at him.

"Yes, five of us meet and draw…let's call them 'challenges,' that's what we—my four friends and I, I mean—always called them. We have a year to complete them. My challenge was to meet, interview, photograph, and write an article about you—well, not you really, but you as Margaret Barnett. We are allowed one clue and mine was Granville. That's what I was doing there that first day. Hell, everyone in town knows I asked about Mrs. Barnett. Remember?"

He talked fast, hoping to convince her before she kicked him out. Because he knew that was probably what she would do. He felt it coming any moment.

Tali was shaking. She couldn't help herself. What she wanted to do was join her friend on the sofa. But this man would never see her cry. "By hook or crook, right? It didn't matter to you who you hurt along the way, did it?"

She glanced over at Lily.

His eyes never left Tali's face.

"Yeah, what about me?" Lily interjected between sobs. "I thought you loved me!"

"Did I ever tell you that?" Brent asked gently. "Did I?"

"Well…no…I guess not," she had to admit.

"Did I ever promise you anything?"

"Well…no. But I thought…oh!" She jumped up and ran from the room.

"You're all she could talk about this last month. Only I thought your name was Michael. I had no idea you were the same man."

"It is Michael," Brent responded. "Brent Michael."

It sounded as lame to him as it did to her.

Tali was so furious she couldn't think. She knew she should demand that he leave, but she hesitated for some reason.

That gave him an opportunity to speak.

"I wasn't planning on falling in love with a beautiful

young lady named Tali. Hell, I've never been in love before in my life. I've been with women, yes. I've dated plenty. But I've never loved even one of them. And I love you, Tali, very, very much."

She drew in her breath. She was in danger of weakening. Her love for this man outweighed anything. But she had her pride. If she gave in now…

"But it didn't stop you from publishing the article about me, did it?"

"Yes, it did, Tali. Yes, I wrote it. I managed to get the photos. I won't say how, but it was by 'hook and crook' as you called it. I sat down one evening and wrote the article, then rewrote it over the next two days, even after I recognized you in the stills. I recognized you by that ring of yours."

He nodded toward her right hand.

She reached over to her finger, rubbing the ring.

"Then I had the face enlarged and couldn't believe it. I was stunned. I loved you as Tali. I wasn't at all prepared for you to be Mrs. Barnett, although enough clues had been there all along. I was just always so aware of your presence in Granville as Tali that nothing else fell into place."

He ran his hand through his hair, shaking his head. Tali wanted to reach up and run her fingers through his hair, also.

Stop thinking like that, she scolded herself.

"After I wrote the article, I realized I couldn't do that to you. I knew you would never forgive me." He paused, hoping she would respond to the hint for forgiveness. He hoped that she would say, of course, she forgave him. But it was too much to hope for. When she didn't say anything, he continued. "I decided the money I would win just wasn't worth it."

"The money you would get from selling the article to that rag?"

"Oh, no. The winner or winners in our little game would split $50,000. You see, each of us had to put in $10,000 at the beginning to be able to play. I've won some and lost some over the years. And I didn't sell it. I put it in a drawer in my apartment. Then my place was robbed about a month ago. I gave a list of things to the police, jewelry and such, but it didn't occur to me to look in the middle drawer of my roll-top desk. After all, it usually only held pens, a stapler, and scotch tape, that sort of thing. It wasn't until after the article was published that I checked the drawer. Sure enough, the brown manila envelope containing the article and photos was gone. I couldn't believe it. Either someone broke in to take the article, and I know who it would be, or the thief saw it and realized what he had."

"Do you hear yourself? Do you?" Tali asked. "You spied on me, yes?"

"Yes," he admitted. He spread his hands. "On Mrs. Barnett. I didn't know you were Mrs. Barnett, or that Mrs. Barnett would turn out to be you—"

"But you still wrote the article, anyway."

He shrugged.

"Then you say you didn't submit it, someone broke into your apartment and stole it. How many thieves do we know who steal articles? Then there's the idea of some sort of game."

"It started out as a game, yes. Look—" He reached inside his pocket and brought out his wallet. He pulled out four business cards. "Here," he said. He held them out toward her. She did not reach out to take them from him so he tossed them onto her desk. "There. Those guys are friends of mine. Call them. They'll tell you about the game, how it's been going on for years. Tali, I love you. I love you as Tali, as Mrs. Barnett, or whoever. You must believe me that I never intended things to go this way, not after I fell in love with you. At least not after I admitted to myself I loved you. And it took a while for me to admit that, believe me."

He smiled.

She did not return the smile.

"Why don't I believe you?" she asked.

She wanted to believe him. She wanted to believe that he had fallen in love with her as Tali, a simple country girl. She had chosen to remain out of the dating game because she was afraid she would not know the difference in whether a man loved her for herself or whether he was after her position and wealth. She had fallen in love with Brent because she believed he loved her as Tali.

"I asked you something once and you danced around the answer. I'm going to ask you again and I want the truth. Who and what are you?" She still had not heard back from her detective agency.

When he told her who he was, what he owned, she gasped.

"So, you see, I don't need the money. And you fell in love with me, not knowing who I am or what I possess. You do love me, don't you, Tali?"

He had lowered his voice. It was soft and wooing, enticing her to believe him.

She almost gave in. She almost walked around the desk to throw herself in his arms.

Almost.

Instead, she never moved. "There are too many deceptions, Brent. I don't know who you are or what you do or even what you want from me. Please leave. Please leave and don't come back. Ever. Don't call. What is it they say? 'Don't call me, I'll call you.'"

Her voice was cold. It sent chills down his spine.

"Is that really the way you want it?"

"Yes."

"Then, so be it!"

He straightened, his neck stiffened as she told him to leave. He would not beg her. He would not beg for a further audience or forgiveness.

She was so cold, so unresponsive. How did he ever

think he loved this cold fish, this shell of a woman? He turned and walked out of the office, his head held high.

Tali stood motionless as she heard the outer door close.

All was silent. Lily must have fled to her apartment. There was not a sound from the temp in the outer office.

Tali told herself she had done the best thing, the right thing. She never wanted to see him again.

Her whole body sagged and she sat down hard in her chair. All the energy was gone from her. She felt like a limp rag.

She put her head down in her arms on the desk and wept.

Chapter 27

Lily had suffered, though. She had cried and cried. She had almost convinced herself that she had fallen in love with Brent. Or with Michael. Or whatever his name was.

Only after numerous talks with Tali, each of them baring their souls to the other, did Lily come to realize that it was Brent and Tali who belonged together.

Lily had to admit he had never promised her anything, not by word or deed. She had just let herself fantasize about him, that's all. But she was less forgiving about the deceptions than Tali was. Maybe that was a part of Tali's love for him.

Lily would get over him.

It was different with Tali. She could not keep Brent out

of her thoughts. One day, she reached inside her desk and pulled out the business cards he had tossed at her. She would find out if what he said about the game was true.

A mere phone call would not do. Phone lines could go anywhere and proved nothing. She called the number on one of the cards—a financial planner with offices not too far from her own. It was the only local address. The other cards gave addresses in New York, Paris, Hong Kong, Los Angeles, and Denver.

She called that day and was told she could come the next day.

So here she was, looking up at the Franklin Financial Center. She took a deep breath and went through the front door.

Thomas Franklin was expecting her.

As she stepped through the door to his office, he rose to meet her and walked around his desk. He was visibly surprised at her presence.

He reached out and took the hand she offered.

She was dressed in a fashionable business suit with short shirt, matching heels and hat. She knew what he was thinking. She smiled, which produced a reciprocal smile from him. "I know. You were expecting someone older. Right?"

"Well, yes, come to mention it. Even though I saw the article about you that first night, I really didn't look too closely at it. Sorry." He managed to look sheepish. "I always had the impression that Mrs. Barnett was an older woman. And is it…Mrs…Barnett?"

"No, it isn't," she responded.

"Please, have a seat," he said, as he gestured toward a chair on the client side of his desk. He took the chair next to her, facing her. Somehow, he knew not to go around and sit behind his desk. He could not imagine this to be a business call. "Would you like some coffee? A water, perhaps?"

"No, thank you," she replied. "I only want to take a few minutes of your time. I can imagine what a busy man you are."

Thomas Franklin thought she could take as much of his time as she liked. He wondered why Margaret Barnett had asked to meet with him personally. He had, of course, agreed to see her. Who would not have? But he couldn't imagine her needing any financial advice from him. But stranger things had happened.

"And what can I help you with, Ms. Barnett?"

"Brent Walker," she replied simply.

"Brent? What about him?" he asked.

She could tell he was surprised at the name.

Why was this woman wanting to know about Brent? Surely she had the same *Dun & Bradstreet* and *AM Best* sources that he did. How did she know he was his friend?

"He is a personal friend of yours?" she asked

"Yes," he admitted. He was getting more and more curious as to why she was here.

"He told me to ask you about 'the game.' A game that five of you have played for years now, where you submit…challenges…I think he called them, for each of you to choose and solve. Once a year, he said."

"He told you about our game?"

"Was it a secret?" she asked.

"Well, no, not in the sense you usually think a secret is. It was just usually between the five of us, some spouses, of course, but not the general public, if you know what I mean."

She nodded. She made an instinctive decision to trust this man. Knowing Brent as she did, his choice of friends would be trustworthy. She told him briefly about how they met, she as Tali, Brent not knowing who she was. Everything. She even confessed how much she loved Brent, and he loved her, yet they had parted, at her request.

"At least that explains everything," he said as she finished.

"And what is that?" she asked.

"The way he's been acting for the last month," he responded. "I even asked him once if he was in love, and he looked startled. He didn't respond, though. Now I know he was—er—is."

"So, the bottom line of why I came here today is to see if what he said about the game was the truth," Tali continued.

"Yes, it is. In fact, of all the men you could have chosen to visit, I'm the one who put the assignment about you in the game. Maybe because you are in the same city, maybe some other reason. Frankly, I've forgotten why I did it now. But it was true. And I will assure you of one thing."

"What's that?" she asked.

"If Brent has fallen as madly and deeply in love with you as I think he has and as you truly believe he has, then he did not submit that article. He would not have done that to you, or to your friends and family in Granville. Not after he got to know you.

"You see," he continued, "a lot of people think he is ruthless in business, and I have to admit I have seen him make some pretty daring deals. But he also has a very compassionate, very loving side to him that not many people see. I was his roommate in college, though, and I know him. And if he loved you a month ago, you can believe he still loves you this very day."

"But I told him to go away and never come back."

"He won't, then."

She looked up at him.

He thought he saw tears in her eyes. "He has a lot of pride. He's also stubborn. You'll have to go to him first. If you're not willing to do that, then you'll both never experience the true love you've found with each other. And believe me, life will go on, but it will never be the same. You will always know something is missing."

She sat still, just looking him straight in the face. He

wasn't very old. No older than Brent. "You sound so wise. So experienced," she said.

"Yeah. Experienced. I should have married my college sweetheart, but for reasons I won't go into now, I lost her. But not a minute of the day goes by I don't think of her and how much I still love her."

Why was he telling this woman this? He had never told anyone before. Was it because of her great love for his best friend? Or because he did not want Brent to lose his chance at true love?

"Are you married?" she asked, unexpectedly.

"Yes, I am," he answered.

She could tell by the way he replied he wasn't very happy.

"Is your college sweetheart married?"

"No, she's never married."

Tali made a deliberate display of looking around at his office, at his possessions. "They aren't worth it, you know," she said, softly. "If you're worried about divorcing your wife because you will lose all this—" She waved her hand around at the room. "—then do it, anyway. Go to your true love and love her so completely, so deeply, for the rest of your life that you will never regret giving up material things. Love is the most important thing."

She rose and extended her hand. He had risen when she did. He took her hand and held it for a few seconds.

He knew why and how Brent could love her so much.

"Are you going to follow our own advice?" he asked.

"Yes, I am," she answered. "And thank you for helping me."

"No," he said. "Thank you."

She left the building knowing what she had to do.

As soon as she had left his office, Franklin picked up the phone.

His attorney could see him right away.

Franklin needed to feel loved again.

Chapter 28

Tali stretched out in the chair, adjusting her hat. She was sitting beside the pool. This island was her favorite place. And because she always registered in another name, no one identified her with the publishing magnate.

She needed the peace and quiet of this place and time. After the traumatic confrontation with Brent, her nerves were raw. Her whole body was on edge.

She had spent three glorious weeks just lying out on the beach, swimming, relaxing and reading. She received no phone calls, which was the way she wanted it. Although she never got many in Granville, now too many people knew about her place there.

They knew—and she had thought it was thanks to

Brent Walker. Although he swore to her that he did not "leak" the information of her "alter ego," as one of the tabloids put it, she had not believed him. Somehow, it had been revealed, and he had seemed, to her, to be the most likely suspect for having done so.

Hadn't that been his purpose from the beginning? To interview her, to reveal things about her to the public that no one had known before? To be the first to "get to her."

And to think she had believed that he had loved her—had loved her as Tali, a small town girl of modest means. She thought she had finally found "Mr. Right," who would love her for herself and not for her riches.

How wrong she had been! And, yet, didn't her heart still tell her something different? Her heart still betrayed her. She loved him! It was that simple. She loved him as she had never loved anyone before and knew she never would again.

But words had been spoken in anger that could not be recalled. Those words had driven him away. She would never forget the set of his jaw as he listened to her and the stiffness of his back as he had turned from her and walked away, his head held high. He had walked out of her life.

He had not slammed the door, as she had expected. Instead, he had turned, put his hand on the knob, and given her one long, last look, before gently shutting the door. Shutting himself out of her life.

A stifling silence had engulfed her as she stood behind

her desk, staring at the closed door, at the spot where she last saw him. His image seemed to be etched on the door itself.

It had been a month now, and she had not heard from him. Did she really expect to? He had promised never to bother her again, as Tali or Mrs. Barnett. Still, she had expected something from him, after her note to him, apologizing for accusing him of the tabloid piece. One of her newspaper sources had investigated the matter for her and had uncovered the culprit. This man didn't even know Brent, but he had realized what he saw when he robbed his apartment. A person in her organization—duly terminated now—had also leaked personal information to a "yellow-dog" journalist who had put the information together and used Brent's name as the author.

There was hope when her note did not return to her in the mail. So, someone had received it, at least. She had sent it certified, return receipt. The green receipt had come back to her. True, the signature was unreadable, but someone at his address had signed for it.

She had thought of him continually the past month, and now she had only two more days here. She could have stayed here, but here was not reality—not her reality. She had to get back into life, live again.

But it was hard trying to imagine a life or world without Brent in it.

Chapter 29

Every morning, as he dressed, Brent looked at the envelope from Tali, still untouched and unopened, with the green certified mail strips on it. His housekeeper had signed for it, as she was authorized to do.

But he had not opened it.

Why should he let her abuse and malign him more than she already had? Tali had not even given him the time or opportunity to explain anything in that last meeting with her.

Oh, that last meeting. She was beautiful when she was angry, her temper all but uncontrollable, although she'd tried valiantly to stay calm.

In cold, impersonal tones, she had told him exactly what she thought of him at that point. No wonder, he had thought, she had been able to keep reins on her many organizations. Past the first few sentences, he simply shut up and listened.

He wasn't going to beg her to listen. He had too much pride for that. If she was that unreasonable, then, fine, that was it. How could anyone live with a woman like that? Why did he even think he could?

It would be hell!

But he had seen another side of Tali that would also be heaven.

He had propped the envelope up on his dresser and had looked at it for a month now. Several times, he had caught himself starting to reach for it, wanting to open it, but had stopped himself. Why should he be interested, now, in anything she had to say?

But he *was* interested. He had to admit that. As much as he had wanted to stay angry with her, to have a reason to hate and forget her, he just simply had not been able to.

Her beautiful face, hair, smile had been just below the surface of every thought he had this past month. He could hear her joyous laughter and feel her beautifully smooth skin. Most of all, he could taste her and feel her kiss on his lips. At those times, more than any other, he knew he loved her. He loved her completely, unconditionally.

It didn't matter what she had said to him. He knew he would forgive anything, if only he had her love again.

This time, when he reached for the letter, he found it in

his hand. He held it for a few long minutes.

"Oh, what the hell!" he said, as he tore it open. "I'm just a glutton for punishment!"

He stood stunned as he began reading the handwritten letter inside.

Tali was apologizing, explaining herself.

He forgot all the words that he had just read when he came to the last sentence she had written:

> *I love you more than anything, more than life itself. I can admit that now—now that it's too late. I know you'll never forgive me for what I said to you. How can I expect you to? But I do ask your forgiveness for everything I've done to hurt you.*
>
> *I will always love you.*
> *Love, Tali*

She loved him! She didn't hate him, didn't mean the things she had said! As long as she loved him, they could work everything out.

He was on the phone to Tali in a minute, with the letter still in his hand. He called on her private line, which went directly to her desk.

When Lily answered, he almost hesitated, almost hung up the phone. Lily had once been an ally. He could only hope she would help him now.

It took some convincing, but Lily finally told him

where Tali was. But she would only tell him the place, not the name of the hotel or number.

His next call was to the airlines. Surely, he could find her. The island she went to was not that big.

He had to hurry. Although she wasn't due back for three days, that was too risky. She could decide to come home early. He preferred to surprise her there.

ↄ৺ↄ

For two days, he had searched every hotel and motel on this island for Tali. She had obviously registered in another name, so he had no choice but to try to watch each place. The problem, of course, was that he could always be watching one place whenever she was outside another.

How crazy this was. The odds against just spotting her, in all these crowds, were astronomical.

But he would try anything to find her. A call to Lily assured him that she was still here. But she had been given strict orders not to tell anyone where she was. And although Lily knew how much Tali loved this man, her loyalty to her friend prevented her from telling him her exact location.

So, here he was, standing at the edge of the pool area. He had checked this resort when he first arrived, just on a hunch, but had not located Tali. Even photos of her brought shakes of the head from most people.

That reminded him of the locals in Granville. Were these people protecting her, also?

He looked around. This place seemed like her type of place.

He had just straightened himself up from leaning on a wall, ready to leave, when a door opening halfway down the row of bungalows caught his attention.

He was surprised when Tali stepped out. He lost no time in heading that way. The door had not shut behind her. She stepped back into the room, leaving the door wide open. She was bent over, getting something out of a drawer when he stepped through the door.

"You shouldn't leave your door open, you know. There's no telling who might come in."

"Brent!" she breathed, her whole face lighting up with pleasure at the sight of him. Her smile was like a breath of air to him. She had taken a step backward, her hand on her chest. "What are you doing here?"

"I just came to tell you how much I love you. I love Tali, Margaret Matilda, and Mrs. Barnett so much it hurts. This past month has been an absolute hell without you. Please let me explain everything, Tali. My world is nothing without you!"

He looked so forlorn, so helpless, her heart melted within her. He looked as if he had not had a good night's sleep in a long time, as well he hadn't.

"There's nothing to explain," she responded. "There's only our love. Please forgive me for saying such awful things to you. I've been so miserable, too, I thought I didn't want to go on living. And I don't want to go on living without you. I love you so much!"

By the time she had finished speaking, his long legs had carried him across the room to her. He reached out and gathered her into his arms, breathing deeply of her perfume. He ran his fingers through her hair, growing dizzy with the softness of it.

She held him tight, as if she were afraid she would lose him again.

He picked her up in his arms and took a few steps backward, reaching his foot out at the same time.

This time, with a soft click, the door shut behind them.

END

About the Author

Mary Jane Bryan is a graduate of Missouri State University (SEMO), Cape Girardeau, Missouri, with a BS in Business Administration/General Management and a graduate of Three Rivers Community College, Poplar Bluff, Missouri, with an AA in General Studies.

Bryan is strong believer in women as entrepreneurs and managers, and she is a past creator and owner of Jane's Muppets. She is a past member of Toastmasters International, which is an excellent resource for creative writing and presentation, receiving critiques and advice as needed. A past resident of Ecuador, Bryan now currently resides in Farmington, Missouri, with her husband, Peter, and their cat, Cookie.